Engglishhh©

Praise for *Mumbai Noir*

'This is a very precious collection ... If one takes the time and the effort to read between the lines, one might even chance upon that odd moment of silence'

—*The Hindu*

'Tyrewala's insightful introduction greatly enhances the reading experience ... The collection is astonishingly diverse ... It might provide a fictional contrast to Katherine Boo's *Behind the Beautiful Forevers*'

—*Library Journal* (Starred review)

'Most of the 14 short stories ... draw inspiration from the criminal networks and the sordid underbelly the city is infamous for ... Armchair travellers will find plenty of amusement in touring the seedier parts of this island city in perfect safety'

—*Publishers Weekly*

Praise for *No God in Sight*

'This is a sparkling debut, a first novel of confidence, verve and high talent, written with a wit, light touch and deep humanity which brings its world to vivid, memorable life'

—Salman Rushdie

'A bullet train of a novel, scintillating with bursts of energy and scathing humour as it streaks through the Bombay landscape—the kind of book you will want to press on all your acquaintances and insist they read it'

—Manil Suri

'This is Altaf Tyrewala's first novel but he plays with form with the self-assurance of a seasoned writer. With *No God in Sight* you are in a Bunuelesque world, an unsettling relay race in which the baton is passed on from one character to another and one story to another till you come full circle'

—Kiran Nagarkar

'Kudos to Altaf Tyrewala for returning the novel to its original, glorious function: giving a name to the city's teeming masses, turning faces into individuals'

—Amitava Kumar

First published in hardback in India in 2014 by Fourth Estate
An imprint of HarperCollins *Publishers* India

Building 10, Tower A, 4th Floor, DLF Cyber City, Phase II,
Gurugram Haryana – 122002, India
www.harpercollins.co.in

ISBN: 978-93-5029-753-7

2 4 6 8 10 9 7 5 3 1

Typeset in Adobe Arabic 14/14.3
Jojy Philip, New Delhi 110 015

Printed and bound at
MicroPrints India, New Delhi

Engglishhh©

FICTIONAL DISPATCHES FROM A HYPERREAL NATION

ALTAF TYREWALA

FOURTH ESTATE • *New Delhi*

In memory of
New and Secondhand Bookshop
(Dhobi Talao, Mumbai)
1905–2011

Contents

New and Second-hand

LITERACY is overrated. I haven't read a book in years and I'm doing fine, thank you. Just because I sell books for a living doesn't mean I have to know what's in them. I'm like a chemist. I'd be dead or very, very sick if I sampled my own products. That's how I see books anyway, as remedies for ailing minds; papery crutches for doddering intellects that are struggling to get a grip on the world.

I was a voracious reader in my youth. Books are for the young. The right tome at an early age can forever shape the course of a person's life. And the wrong books? The wrong books will keep you searching forever. I must confess, it's these latter books that keep booksellers in the business.

I don't intend to reveal my identity or the location or name of my bookshop. I have much to say about books and about people who read, write, publish and sell them. Most of what I have to say is unpleasant, and I will probably end up embarrassing a lot of people, not least myself. Lord knows I don't need more enemies, or more humiliation. Be that as it may, there are several details that I cannot withhold, if I am to make this confession of sorts have some balls of its own. The last thing the world needs is another lily-livered volume. I am surrounded all day by these failed attempts: copies of handsomely jacketed and tediously conceived tomes that have been sitting on my store's shelves for years, gathering dust, waiting in vain for that one reader who will buy into their promise of shining a spotlight onto some dark or unexplored aspect of our shared reality. I am tempted to become a reader again just so these obsolete books can fulfil their intended destiny one last time before being sold by the kilo to the neighbourhood paper-recycling shop.

It's not like I don't read at all. Who can avoid content these days? It comes at us in a three-sixty-degree attack. Newspapers, magazines, catalogues, brochures, billboards, pamphlets, ticker tapes, and my favourite bugbear: the Internet. Did people always have so much to say? Maybe they did, and maybe they just didn't have a way to get their point across. Now, of course, it's a free-for-all. Anyone with half a command over the language and any old, remotely interesting idea can have a book or blog to their name. I'd like to rectify my earlier chemist analogy. Books aren't like remedies to ailments, they are the ailments themselves; unwholesome products of unquiet minds that keep psychological imbalances in currency. By extension, I suppose that makes me a very dangerous businessman.

I stock mostly second-hand books. And by that I am referring to the history of ownership of my goods. As to the newness of the ideas they contain, I suppose all books are second-hand, even the ones sitting pretty on the shelves of spiffy air-conditioned bookstores—you know the types, with the attached cafés and gift shops.

Reading used to be a step away from renunciation. Now it is another excuse to pick up unattractive lovers. I am approached by publishers all the time, practically commanding me to host a book launch in my store. I take perverse delight in saying no. I am also against self-important book clubs and reading groups that want to turn my establishment into some sort of weekend living room for their weird literature symposiums. I decided to be a bit accommodating once and allowed a book discussion on my premises. It was a fiasco. Two men came to blows. My employees had to intervene. Coffee cups were smashed and a royal mess was made. Can't remember the author responsible for the fracas. Definitely wasn't Sartre or Borges. It's hard to fight over something you don't understand.

Most of my stocks are sourced from the collections of recently deceased people, or from libraries that are shutting shop, or from people who are going abroad. Given the limited shelf space, the influx of a sizeable book collection shapes the character of my modest shop for several weeks, until new books replace the old ones. We are currently undergoing a mixed-bag phase of sorts, thanks to the insanely eclectic book collection of a renowned Bharatanatyam dancer. Her identity will be obvious to those in the know. She fled the country after right-wingers took offence at one of her performances. Her three children say it's doubtful their mother can or will ever want to return to this spiteful, atavistic nation of hers (mine, ours). At the dancer's massive sea-facing suburban flat, several walls of which were decorated with their absent owner's photos showing her bedecked in Bharatanatyam regalia, I was quite surprised to find that almost half of her book collection was from my store.

There's no mistaking one of my books. The back page has a coded notation in green pencil indicating the date the entire lot was purchased on and average cost of the books in that lot. It looks something like this: DEPP-FCPU. But in green. The date is there for sentimental reasons. When I go through my stocks or stumble upon a book somewhere that was once in my store, I like to be able to tell when that particular book entered the orbit of my commercial enterprise. Noting the average cost serves as a ready reckoner for times when I'm faced with hard bargainers—I won't part with a book for less than twice the average cost of the lot it belongs to. I guard my code's method with a spy-like paranoia. Successive batches of employees have tried hard to decipher it. It's their favourite pastime when business is slack. Thankfully, the sort of person who comes to work at a second-hand bookshop isn't the brightest of the lot. I didn't mean to be so guarded with my uncomplicated code. Now it's become a running tradition. My unchallenged expertise over my code makes me feel like the last speaker of an ancient tongue that will die with my death.

My shop, in all probability, will wind up after I'm gone—unless a successor springs forth from my much-abused loins, or from the extended family. I meant to marry. I meant to have a wife and kids and a well-oiled household like all other square men in the books business. I doomed myself by shopping around too much. I thought the more women I sampled, the closer it would get me to the one woman I was destined to be with. Instead, the more I looked, the more I found every woman to be like every other. By my late thirties, driven to desperation, I was ready to make do. But women sensed this and were repelled. Even women who would've settled for anyone at all demurred when it came to me. In my mid-forties, now, I've made peace with my partnerless existence. All I want is to be left alone—with my business, my TV dinners and my nightly routine of pre-sleep self-pleasuring. It's the sort of self-contained life I endured during my pre-sexual student days. If only someone had told me then that I needn't bother sampling the apple, that I am the best lover I will ever find.

In the initial years of my business, I nursed the pompous belief that it was my duty to shape my clients' literary tastes. I thought my carefully vetted philosophy, literature and art sections were the pride of my shop, but how did that matter? Most customers would zoom straight to the thriller and romance racks. They still do. It made my blood boil. For several years I banished mass-market potboilers or anything resembling them from my store. Thanks to my heroic stand against popular tastes, I became famous among a small band of the city's literary aesthetes. While my love life blossomed because of my renowned snootiness, my business suffered. I call it my shop's art-house era, in deference to the Hindi film industry's brief flirtation with cinéma-vérité in the early 1980s, an ascetic phase that was brought to an abrupt end with the arrival of superstar-driven blockbusters.

My own shop's anti-best-seller stance was reversed the day I fell in love with a best-selling novelist. Our romance soured after four months of hectic and rather stressful coupling. If being with a hack like her could be so strenuous, I shudder to imagine the nightmare of keeping up with a serious author. After we were through, I suppose I should've reintroduced my store's anti-best-seller policy to spite my ex-best-selling girlfriend. But after several years of making do with break-even, now that I'd reopened my doors to the literary equivalent of burgers and fries, I had become attached to the spike in footfalls and to the happy buzz of a busy bookshop. I can no longer afford to disdain profitability. I am not getting any younger.

To safeguard against the possibility of geriatric poverty, I invest in rare and old books the way most people invest in their children. At least my investments won't turn around and bite the hand that paid for them. I keep scores of these precious books individually plastic-wrapped in a steel cupboard in my bedroom. I reshuffle them once every month, because otherwise books have a way of packing into each other like layers of mud. When I do the monthly airing, I invariably come across at least one or two books that no longer seem worthy of being hoarded in the haloed space of the cupboard. Maybe in the interim period I've found an even older edition, or maybe the author of an autographed copy has finally died to much less public lamentation than I had anticipated. I suppose every investment carries with it an implicit risk. My biggest fear is that by the time I'm ready to start selling my rare possessions, the world will no longer deem them worth the price I plan to quote. Old things, books included, will always have a market. It's the only way we can hope to interpret the past—by possessing its debris. It remains to be seen, however, if people will be willing to pay enough for that debris to sustain an old retired second-hand bookseller.

As far as I can help it, I never refuse used books that come my way, unless they are in unsaleable condition, or are of arcane or dubious nature, or if the seller is being unreasonable with the price. Despite my perennial readiness to purchase books, I sometimes undergo long stretches when nothing is being offered for sale. What can be more pleasurable to a businessman than to watch his stocks dwindle before his very eyes? When bald patches begin to appear on my shelves, it is time to take matters into my own hands. I bundle up a few thousand rupees, leave the store to my employees and hit the streets.

Despite frequent crackdowns by the authorities, Mumbai's footpath economy remains a guilty pleasure for the city's denizens. Hawkers and vendors are like flies that settle back no matter how many times they've been driven out. The municipality can do zilch. The resilience of Mumbai's unorganized (and illegal) retail sector gives citizens access to laughably cheap food, clothes, shoes, accessories and, most pertinently for me, books.

To anyone who still nurses ambitions of penning a book, I recommend a visit to one of Mumbai's roadside bookstalls. Here plastic sheets are spread out on pavements and strewn on them are hundreds of books, just inches from the mud-splattered shoes and sandals of pedestrians click-clacking by indifferently. New York editions, London editions, Sydney editions and New Delhi editions, all thrown together in their wretched unwantedness. No matter where you live or what you write about, no matter how many millions of pounds you receive as an advance or how much of a big shot your agent might be, there is nothing you can do to prevent your book from trickling down to Mumbai's unforgiving streets. You can, however, do something to rescue your book once it has landed on Mumbai's footpaths. It isn't easy, it takes monumental patience and back-breaking effort, and you're as likely to fail as you are to succeed. But it's doable. The secret to ensuring that your book, having landed up on Mumbai's pavements, doesn't stay there for too long is this: write a stupendous book. A book so magnificent that it will be picked up regardless of the dust and bird droppings sullying its cover, and irrespective of the funny smell emanating from its yellowed pages. When I go book shopping to replenish my stocks, I think of myself as the saviour of all these excellent, deeply felt and well-written works of art—both highbrow and lowbrow, fiction and non-fiction—that landed up by the side of the street for no fault of theirs. Most stall owners don't see me as competition. They are grateful for my bulk purchases. I exploit their desperation and their ignorance by picking up gems for a song.

For a few days after I have gone on one of my shopping sprees, the space behind my counter resembles a literary infirmary. Paperbacks and hardcovers lie around in various states of disrepair, awaiting healing attention from me or one of my employees. The books I buy off the street are often in dire condition, and need to be brought back from the brink of disintegration before they are fit enough to be coded and placed on my shelves.

I won't be able to tell you what books I have in my store. I keep no catalogue, no computerized list. Once something has been shelved in its particular section, it becomes a dull memory, more an object of fuzzy intuition than of active intellect. Even if I or my employees knew where a particular book was, we wouldn't want to tell you. A reader may come looking for Naipaul's biography by French, and might walk out with that and with Theroux's scandalous account of his friendship with Naipaul. Such are the incidental joys of browsing. It takes a particular sort of personality to delight in the unexpected find, to take relish in stumbling upon something while seeking something else. I am sad to report that such a personality, receptive to serendipity, is now on the wane.

The current lot of customers are turned off by my inability to say for certain whether I have the book they want. They are alarmed when I invite them to look around the store. How miserable it must be to want *only* what one wants. I don't remember people being so disinterested in the unfamiliar. Folks these days seem annoyed when they encounter something that they haven't already cross-checked, as if the perpetually connected sizzle of their web-wired lives precludes the possibility of anything still remaining unknown.

Some of the books in my shop are so old, and have been out of print for so long, I doubt that their authors—provided they are still alive—even remember them. It amazes me how some of these books were ever allowed to exist. The scholarship of previous generations seems so quaint in retrospect. To imagine that men and women of earlier eras devoted their entire lives studying, for instance, the effects of electricity on human souls!

'I hope your bookshop never shuts down.' Every day, at least two customers say this to me with a sad sigh, while shelling out peanuts for their purchases. The wealth of these customers is evident from their oversized phones and leather-bound tablets, their branded wallets and handbags, the crisply casual clothing. I call them the Lamenters of Fading Bombay. They grieve the closing down of Irani cafés. They rage against the phasing out of Padmini taxis. They claim to scour through Chor Bazaar on their days off. They fetishize the doddering, the decaying and the outdated, while ensuring that nothing and no one threatens their state of belonging to the swanky, the newly constructed and state-of-the-art.

I have news for these bleeding-heart lamenters. I am trying to stave off the owner of a busy grade IV restaurant next to my bookshop. He wants to expand. He knows that I have been on the verge of bankruptcy since the time I began this bookshop on these premises I inherited from my father. It is only a matter of time before the restaurateur makes me the proverbial offer I can't refuse. And then there will be one more Fading Bombay institution for the Lamenters to converge on, to photograph and eulogize on their social media postings. I know how I am expected to behave during those final months. Shoulders hunched in defeat. A permanent expression of regret tinged with just a touch of sadness, but no overt expression of grief, because intense emotions scare the lamenters; it challenges them to do something, when all they want is to flutter about and document an unfolding commercial tragedy.

With the sale of the premises, I will be richer than I have ever been in my entire life. Mumbai's real estate is a once-in-a-lifetime cheque which, once cashed, can see a whole family to the end of its days. This city offers enough diversions to keep the financially well off perennially occupied. I will be spoiled for choice: cricket matches, film, music and food festivals, and, if nothing else, there will always be some Fading Bombay business that will have just announced its closure, giving idlers like me an excuse to patronize it, to commiserate with its broken owners. I may offer to buy a piece of furniture from the establishment as a keepsake, a chair maybe, or a wall clock. It will be one more piece of junk to adorn my overcrowded inherited home, which I will eventually sell as well, and move to a cheaper city, fading away from this city like everything else, like everybody else.

Engglishhh©

HISTORY has been rewritten. It is now hsstroy. Nothing will be the same again. (Not even 'nothing', which is now noohing.)

Welcome to Engglishhh©, an antidote to the world's most inauspiciously spelled language.

Compiled by a team of seventeen numerologists after years of fevered calculations, Engglishhh© contains more than 200,000 English words respelled in accordance with ancient Indo-Puranic principles. Engglishhh© cures the ill effects of English, bestowing on its users positive vibrations and fruitful karmic results.

The compilation has been alphabetized for easy referencing. From nouns, verbs, adjectives, adverbs and articles to names of continents, countries, states, presidents and even Brangelina's children! No facet of the English speaker's world experience has been left unmodified by our resident mahagurus. And so, democracy is now dmoocrcy, colonialism is still colonialism, globalization is gloobliation, and so on.

These are no arbitrary alterations. It took our panel of erudite numerologists, headed by the Bannaruss-based Shi Panddut Rajj Meeshrr, hours of intricate computations and scholarly cross-referencing to amend the unfavourable spelling of each English word.

For a detailed word-by-word numerological analysis, please refer to the five-volume *Guuidee Too Engglishhh©*.

Here are some dazzling illustrations:

The English word Car (3+1+8=12) is represented by the number Twelve, depicted by the image of a one-winged eagle soaring over a city of gold. Good for a kitchen appliance, suicidal for a personal mode of transport.

The Engglishhh© version, Caar (3+1+1+8=13), is a number Thirteen word, ruled by the unseen and as yet unnamed planet between Saturn and Pluto. By thinking of your car as caar, you will observe your social life wither and your mood darken, until you no longer have the will to leave home, and thus you will be protected from fierce road accidents and skyrocketing petrol prices.

In another example, the English word Sex (7+4+1=12) is represented by the number Twelve, depicted by (refer to above paragraph).

Whereas Sssx (7+7+7+8=29), the Engglishhh© version, belongs to number Twenty-nine, the harbinger of bloodshed, disease and painful death, which is how it should be for promiscuous heathens who failed to rise above their beastly natures.

The above instances illustrate the arcane and often audacious reasoning that dictates the alphabetical readjustment of English words. The result is Engglishhh©, the most fortune-fetching and life-altering language in the history of the world!

Here is what Asswin Loopezz (previously Ashwin Lopez), a first year BCom student from Koolkkata (previously Calcutta), says, 'All I want to say is thank you, or rather, thnkk ou to the Engglishhh© dictionary for filling my life with light and wisdom. I am certain the promised results will follow once I have mastered the new spellings.'

Rrrbha Apt (previously Prabha Apte), an aspiring novelist from Atlanta, wrote in saying, 'Engglishhh© hass rejuveenated mmm writtingg. Wiithh Engglishhh© I finaaly hav mmm oon uniquuee sstylee. Eeddittrs caan goo too heel. I ammm nott seekkinnng aadvvnceees oor awwards, buutt meerly the chancee too xpreess. I ammm nverr gooing too stoop writtingg inn Engglishhh©.'

As this last testimony demonstrates, there is a temptation to pass off misspelled words as Engglishhh©, but doing so only results in incoherence and sudden occurrences of severe bad luck. Users of Engglishhh© are advised to invoke this talismanic language with immense reverence and care.

Some frequently asked questions (FAQs) with regard to the usage of Engglishhh©:

Q) Must I also speak in Engglishhh©?

A) Not unless the people you are speaking to know Engglishhh©. Thousands of Engglishhh© words, such as bcase, knwleedge, gst, mxtstast and so on, are unpronounceable. The psychic benefits of Engglishhh© are most acute in the written form.

Q) Fr hwww loong mmmst I mainnnntin mmm uusage oof thiiis lanngug?

A) Eh?

Q) I have been using Engglishhh© for a long time but have observed no noticeable changes in my life. When will Engglishhh© change my life?

A) English, like any form of self-abuse, has a lasting impact on its users' astral bodies. While change may be slow to come, be assured that inside the deepest recesses of your brain's inferior frontal gyrus, a veritable Revolt of 1857 is under way, and this time Engglishhh©, unlike our hapless freedom fighters, will deliver a lasting and humiliating blow to English.

Q) Would history be different if it had been in Engglishhh©?

A) Absolutely. If Swaraj, for example, had been Sswaraaj, India's self-rule would have been genuine and sustained, not the sham republic that has finally come about after decades of independence.

Q) Is there an English-to-Engglishhh© translating software?

A) Yes, there is, and we are in the process of taking legal action against the makers of this illegal programme.

Q) When will you compile Engglishhh© in German?

A) Engglishhh© in any other language will not be Engglishhh©. Please await further notification.

Q) If I disagree with the numerological reassignment of a particular entry in Engglishhh©, may I add or delete alphabets to make the word more suitable to my karmic needs?

A) Idiot has been respelled as dioot for a specific reason (refer to the five-volume *Guuidee Too Engglishhh©*). If you believe your understanding of numerological principles surpasses that of our panel of full-time experts, you are free to tinker around and call yourself an idoot, idit, iidiotttt, or whatever else you wish.

Important don'ts and do nots

- Do not run spellcheck when typing an Engglishhh© document on MS Word.
- Do not use Engglishhh© on the second, eleventh, twentieth and twenty-ninth of the month, or in the years 2010, 2013, 2080 and 4076.
- Engglishhh© must not be used by people with conjunctivitis, diabetes, arthritis, psoriasis and other English-induced diseases.

At the recently held World Social Forum in Tehran, Iran,

Engglishhh© was awarded the Trojan Prize (for Infusion of Perceptual Misunderstanding into a Western Hegemonistic Framework). Roohann Shahha, chief psychic advisor of *Engglishhh*©, accepted the award from Ji Zheng Kha, president of the Trojan Prize Foundation. Mr Shahha's acceptance speech in Engglishhh© received a standing ovation.

Engglishhh© has featured in the 'Top 10 Most Stolen Books at the Frankfurt Book Fair' for seven consecutive years. Evidently, the wise (albeit thieving) Germans consider *Engglishhh*© beyond a price.

Besides several print runs in India, *Engglishhh*© continues to enjoy inexplicable success in Afghanistan, China, Uzbekistan, Latin America and the Middle East.

Perhaps the most poignant news comes from Cuba, where Engglishhh© writing classes have mushroomed throughout the rogue state. In *Engglishhh*©, unfortunately, Cuba has been respelled as Iraq (a number Eleven word, depicted by a bug-eyed ferret on skewers). We apologize to our Cuban readers for this faux pas. Alas, due to numerological compulsions, corrections can only be made in the eleventh edition of *Engglishhh*©, a good decade away. Sorry again.

Quiz time

Q) Identify the English roots of the following words from *Engglishhh*©:

- bush
- kutta
- haraami
- saalaa
- sooar

Q) The following words are yet to be included in *Engglishhh*©. Suggest the most numerologically advantageous amendments to these words, along with your reasoning for the same:

- India
- Dalit
- Muslim
- Jehad
- America
- New Delhi
- Bollywood
- Pakistan

Send in your answers to PO BOX 201, Ahmedabad 21, only between the fourteenth and nineteenth of March 2026. Entries received earlier or later will be burned in a special four-year-long havan commencing on 20 March 2030.

We would now like to introduce, without further ado, the visionary responsible for the phenomenon that is Engglishhh©, our chief psychic advisor and proud recipient of the aforementioned Trojan Prize: Mr Roohann Shahha.

Born as Rohan Shah in pre-liberalization India of 1977, Roohann was your run-of-the-mill dyslexic child. He persisted in misspelling words despite insults from his teachers and severe beatings at the hands of his parents. Dyslexics now have their own schools and even their own blockbuster Bollywood films, but in India in the 1980s, dyslexia was thought to be the symptom of a devilish and rebellious mind.

Using a combination of persistence and bribery, Roohann's parents managed to have their son promoted from class to class, year upon year. But nothing could prevent the boy from failing his board exams. And miserably. With a college education out of the question, Roohann was ordered to start assisting at his uncle's bookshop. It was hoped that being surrounded by products of the intellect might bring about a magical transformation in Roohann's laggardly brain.

The bookshop gave Roohann a headache. The very thought of reading was enough to make him numb. He mocked customers who came looking for best-sellers and English masterpieces. The customers, in turn, mocked Roohann's penchant for mangling the names of authors and book titles. Wraths of Grape. Flies to Lord. George Louis Eliot. Salman Below Saul. Running Rabbit by Up the Dike. And other screw-ups that were symptomatic of a terribly cross-wired brain. Had it not been for a crucial encounter, Roohann might have spent the rest of his life as a two-bit joker working at a cookie-cutter bookshop.

One evening, while taking an order over the phone, Roohann followed protocol by asking the customer to confirm the spelling of his name. The bookshop had already misplaced too many orders thanks to Roohann's infamous spelling abilities.

The customer said his name was Umesh Prakash. 'Spelled u-u-m-e-e-s-h p-r-r-a-k-s-h...'

Roohann was livid. He thought the customer was mocking him. He retorted by saying, 'Sir, I may not know the spelling of Umesh Prakash, but I know it isn't spelled that way. Now please, tell me the correct spelling so I can process your order.'

'Watch your tone, friend,' Uumeesh Prraksh said. 'It's a free country and that's how I spell my name. If you have a problem I can order my books from elsewhere...'

Roohann and Uumeesh chatted for twenty minutes. By the end of the phone call, Roohaan was granted a new lease of life. He had known nothing of the existence of numerology, or that there were people who wilfully misspelled the names they'd been given at birth in the hope that an alphabet more or less would alter their unhappy destinies. Uumeesh put Roohann in touch with his numerological advisor, Dyeepa Maaolti, and the rest, as they say, is hsstroy.

Every alphabet in English has a corresponding number frequency. As a special bonus to our readers, we won't, for a change, refer you to the five-volume *Guuidee Too Engglishhh*©. Here it is, for free, the *Engglishhh*© Alpha-Numerical Easy-Reference Table:

Alphabets	*Corresponding Number*	*Karmic Significance*
WU P L	1 or 9	Duplicity
B R SV	2	Unity
C E XZ	3	Holiness
D F IO	4	Lion's Roar
G JM T	5 or 8	Ill-begotten Wealth
H K NQ	6	Spilled Milk
AY	7	Bee's Sting

As an exercise to pass some time, write down your full name on a piece of paper. Now, under each alphabet, jot down its corresponding number. Add up those numbers. If your name, for instance, is Saddam Hussein, you will find that your first name adds up to Twenty-nine and your last name adds up to Twenty-four. Remember Twenty-nine and ssx—the-harbinger-of-bloodshed-disease-and-painful-death? Malevolence of this magnitude can only be counteracted by a force of overpowering power. What can possibly cancel the ill effects of Twenty-nine? How about something that is represented by three suns? That's right, three bright golden suns, blazing away all traces of darkness and evil. And what number fits the bill? It's Twenty-four, the realm of three suns! Saddam and Hussein, Twenty-nine and Twenty-four, darkness and light, cancelling each other perfectly. A man with such a name was destined to live a bland, ordinary existence; he ought to have been a curio seller in some touristy neighbourhood of Baghdad. How he ended up ruling a country and came to be executed on international television is unfathomable. Sometimes these things just don't add up.

Faced with such paradoxes, Roohann realized that merely altering the spelling of a person's name without also altering the words that propped up this name in a sentence was like cleaning one's backyard while ignoring the mountain of filth continually landsliding onto one's property. What Roohann suggested was beyond mere cosmetic changes to people's names; it was beyond the scope of anything that numerologists had ever thought of or attempted. What Roohann proposed was the foundational rearrangement of the entire framework of the English language as written and understood by billions of people around the world.

Time is testimony to the greatness of Roohann's intuitive vision. But for several initial years, Engglishhh© was little more than the private obsession of a man whose increasingly misspelled letters and emails convinced people that dyslexia had gnarled his brain beyond repair. Little did they know that this 'deranged dyslexic' was plotting the ultimate revenge on a language that had caused him immeasurable humiliation throughout his life.

Thanks to the kind contribution of the Library of Engglishhh© Department at I-bin-Had University in Khirgaztun, we are able to reproduce the first document ever written in Engglishhh©. Circa 1996, it is a poem Roohann composed in honour of a young woman in his building:

My derr Punaita, ths peem isss foor ou:
When I saaat too wriit a peem
Th woords wooulldn't cme
When the didd the wooulldn't rhhym
When the rhhymeed the maad n seensee
Lik aaa red rose ii aaa blaak annd whit fiilmmm
Lik aaa rinbow ii aaa scccorchin sk
Lik msc frm soomewh ii th ded off niiigt
Gorges mirraclees impssble too expln
When I saaat too wriit a peem I kew
Ll I haad too doo waas dscrb ou

In an interview to *New Age Find* magazine in 2004, Mrs Punaita Roohann Shahha describes her initial reaction on coming face-to-face with Engglishhh©: 'I got Roohann's poem via a friend in the building. When I read it, I was like, what is this nonsense. I couldn't understand a thing. The guy had changed my name from Puneeta to Punaita, he wrote poem as peem. I thought he was retarded. I put the page away. But… I couldn't get that poem or peem or whatever it was out of my head. I would come back from college and pull it out from under my mattress and just let my eyes wander over the mangled words. Something felt right, it appealed to something beyond my intellect. I felt a light shine through the words, as if their incomprehensibility somehow emphasized their true meaning. Later on, Roohann told me what the English version was and I was floored. But the Engglishhh© peem had a mystical power that English just couldn't match…'

The 'mystical power' that Mrs Shahha alludes to is the ability of auspiciously spelled words to affect readers at a supra-cognitive level. What is the point of being legible and precise when Engglishhh© can help you circumvent lower-level brain functions and target your reader's untapped cognitive mind? All of this is backed by thousands of years of sound Vedic, Indo-Gangetic and Hindu-brahmanic numerological principles. Compare Roohann's above-quoted love poem with its paltry English avatar:

My dear Puneeta,
When I sat to write a poem
The words wouldn't come
When they did they wouldn't rhyme
When they rhymed they made no sense
Like a red rose in a black-and-white film
Like a rainbow in a scorching sky
Like music from somewhere in the dead of night
Gorgeous miracles impossible to explain
When I sat to write a poem I knew
All I had to do was describe you

'Engglishhh© is perfectly suited for our post-Western, post-textual, recessionary world order,' says Mick Urwent, professor of postmodern post-linguistics at the University of Walsingham. 'Since everyone agrees that words have lost their meaning, here is Engglishhh© to formalize a process that began with Bill Clinton's famous query, 'Define "Is"'.

Engglishhh© is the correction of hundreds of years of inauspicious spelling conventions that have flourished due to the ignorance of English-speaking people. It is not the subversion of a language, as some critics of Engglishhh© claim. And it is definitely not a 'conspiracy by neo-communist forces to overthrow the communicative vehicle of Western capitalism'.

Ignore the critics, back-biters and dissenters, and order your copy of *Engglishhh©* today.

Here is Roohann Shahha having the final word-say: 'Engglishhh© maarks t een o Worsteen doomnatnn oof t worllld.

I ha beeen ploootn and wtiing foor t daaay too cm foor many yrss. Oonee dy t whool worllld wiil bea spkng Engglishhh© aannddd we ppl of possst-colinal browwn-skned natiiion wiil ha t laast laaugh. Maark yy woords, whit dvl, maark yy woords!'

Truer words have never been uttered.

An Indian Porn Director's Speech to His Hesitant Leading Lady

SPEECH?!

Speech?!

Don't bloody call it that!

Politicians and chief guests give speeches. Utopians and philosophers give speeches. To get into the underpants of unwilling sweethearts, aroused youths give speeches.

I am a creator, a fanatic of my own aesthetic vision. I can't be bothered coaxing others. Listen, sweety, put on your clothes and get out if you aren't fully convinced. I will reshoot *Laila Does Majnu* with a tougher Laila who won't demand emotional babysitting every time her thighs need oiling.

I don't have the energy to spare, you understand? Don't distract me.

I am striving to salvage our sexuality from the onslaught of Swedish and Hollywood smut lords—those peddlers of the obvious who have us convinced that only Nordic supermen and 38D Barbies can be filmed copulating like hyper-sexual bunnies.

Why? Are our Indian bodies a ball short or a breast less? Are we repulsive or impotent?

Millions of our females enkindle millions of our males vitally enough to spawn a billion-strong nation. People like us are *doing* it. Then why can't we *watch* people like us doing it?

Almost a century ago, Gandhi protested similarly: Our seas are briny; why can't we make salt? Our mills weave cloth; why can't we buy it?

Our people are doing it; so why can't we watch?

Because, my dear, we have been colonized once again, and this time around, by a strain of neo-imperialism unimaginably more lethal, for it is a colonization not of our geography or society but of our carnal imaginations.

As a hormone-gorged adolescent growing up in the heart of the Hindi belt, what were my cues at private moments? Take a guess, my love. Was it Disco Shanti? Thunder-thighs Padma Narayan? *Silk-bleeding-Smitha?*

Ghantaa!

I jerked off to grainy images from *Sec-C, Honeycombs* and the now-defunct *O-Gal*—all foreign magazines procured from second-hand bookshops.

Was it fair to have my fantasies overrun by a race of women I was never going to come within shouting distance of? Was it fair to the local girls I kissed with closed eyes while imagining them to be golden-haired and milky smooth?

Things worsened. After graduation I joined a film institute where seniors had turned the audiovisual room into a playhouse of imported films featuring the women of my dreams in outrageous action with absurdly endowed men.

There we were, a future generation of thespians, directors, cinematographers and scriptwriters. Our cinematic ventures were to shape the spirit of the nation. We were the creative elite the common man would look up to.

But we at the institute were no different from the Indian proletariat. If *they* hankered for imported cheese, we fantasized about foreign cows.

Viewing those films evening after evening (for porn is astonishingly addictive), something within me died. Repeatedly watching foreigners debase themselves, I lost my self-respect as well. I didn't want to be myself. I wished to be that horse-long Caucasian with enough to go around for seven blonde angels, and then some.

My obliteration was complete. The conspiracy of white colonizers had succeeded once again: like crores of subjugated men before me, I too wished to become white. Or at least white enough to seduce a white.

What Swaraj to demand and what Quit India to declare when one's libido is under siege?

Men turn to art when the political is impossible.

And so: *Laila Does Majnu.*

She does him in the bedroom and the bathtub; in an elevator and in the back of a car. Laila does Majnu at a deserted rail track, in a park and inside the restroom of a restaurant. She does him and does him and does him even as end titles roll and thunderstruck audiences file out of theatres.

Intricate nuances will swoop my film from the bottom-rung slush of sleaze to the roaring heights of allegory. For, when Laila does Majnu in the bedroom, they soil—look under you, hot buns—a bedspread printed with the Stars and Stripes. They moisten the back seat of a Mercedes. They violate the lawns of Victoria Garden and then proceed to disgrace the tiles of a McDonald's toilet.

And in the climax—the last of several climaxes—Laila will do Majnu, upright, against a portrait of Her Highness the Queen!

There will be no dialogues; cinemas will only reverberate with the procreative grunts of two brown-skinned specimens fornicating their way to—finally, finally, oh finally!—a truly sovereign India.

For God's sake, can we shoot now?

World Trade Centre

Shankar

'CANAPICHOO!' I yell, raising the *pichoo* to a comic cadence. I swerve into Zahir sir's cubicle with my cup-laden tray. Look at him. Executive of such a big company, sitting in a cubicle the size of my flat, has a car, money, and how does he start his day? Slumped over his desk like a boneless chicken. What Zahir sir needs is a hot cup of: 'Canapichoo!'

Zahir sir raises his head with a jerk. He sneers. He starts to say, 'It's cappuc...' Instead he shakes his head and slides a tea coaster in place to receive the first of many cups of cappuccino—yes, I know it is cappuccino, I say canapichoo because it amuses people. *Everyone* tips a clown.

'Lunch will be taken, sir?' I ask.

Zahir sir breathes out noisily, as if I have requested a loan or something. Not a bad idea, come to think of it. Nah, I'm not short of money. I have enough.

'What's there?' Zahir sir asks.

What's there? What's *not* there? 'Paneer-palak-vegetable-pulao-daal-fry-papad-roti-boondi-raita-gulab-jamun-garlic achaar...' Woohoo!

Zahir sir shakes his head. 'Learn to talk less. Bring a thaalee at one-thirty.'

Beg your pardon, me lord.

In part to annoy Zahir sir and mostly because it's a harmlessly enjoyable quirk, I croak, 'Thaalee!' in my toad voice and swerve out of his cubicle.

I distribute the remaining cups of cappuccino throughout the office. Coffee, coffee, coffee. My favourite too. Why do you think I'm so hyper and sunny? I down a cuppa every hour. Extra strong, extra sweet. No one drinks tea any more. New world, new needs, got to move, move, move, right or wrong?

'Shankar!' the bespectacled guy with hair like a porcupine stands up from behind his computer screen. 'Coffee! Where's my coffee!'

Shaaaat! I forgot that whole side of the office. 'Canapichoo!' And I'm out of the office, down a long corridor lined with shops and offices, up a floor by stairs, down another corridor, and back at the mother station—the canteen.

'Twenty cappacha!' I shout above the canteen owner's head at the illiterate guys in the kitchen. The canteen owner scowls at me. Other waiters who serve other wings of this office complex gather like bees to the hive and yell their orders. The canteen owner scowls at them too. I think the richer these people get, the sadder they pretend to be, so people won't envy them. The canteen owner must rake it in by the thousands every day.

Corridor. Stairs. Corridor.

I distribute cups of coffee on the spiky-haired guy's side of the office.

Like this it goes on every day, coffee all morning, then lunch, then coffee all afternoon, offices to canteen to offices, carrying hundreds of cups of cappuccino, downing a cup whenever I feel sleepy or tired. I've been doing this for nine years now, started when I was nineteen. Will I do this all my life? Yes, most certainly.

I enjoy it all so much. Serving coffee in the mornings, then lunch, then coffee till closing time. Some evenings I don't even want to go home. Home is hot, stifling and crowded. Home is a crammed, violent two-hour train ride away. I want to be in here, in this office complex, forever. Where cool air descends like a blessing from the ceiling. Where the marble floors are swabbed by Housekeeping every two hours. No sweat, no heat, no mess, no depressing thoughts, no sadness. Just breathing easy and working hard.

'Shankar!'

OK, listen, I have to get back to work, it's time for the second round of morning coffee. Go, talk to one of the security guards on the ground floor. I'm sure they'll have a story to tell you.

Manglya

Shankar sent you? Come, come, stand here next to me. Let's chat. I'm bored to death. Today I've been stationed at this seldom-used side entrance, got lots of time to kill.

You got a cigarette? A beedi? *Nothing*?

Lucky you. Your life must be action-packed. That's why no vices. I have some tobacco and white lime, but I'll have it after you're gone. I am forty-six. I love onions with food and I have a chronic gas problem. Wait, don't go! It doesn't smell; never smells. I've broken wind twice since you came; you got to know? No, no? That gas problem and sometimes a sore back. Otherwise, fit like a horse.

Hang on, I have to frisk that visitor.

You won't believe the stuff people carry around with them. Once, a few months ago, I was frisking a man; I passed my hand over his trousers and felt a lump in his side pocket. It couldn't be a bomb, of course I knew that. But the lump felt weird. I asked to see it.

The man said, 'Mind your business. Would I carry a bomb in my pocket?' I knew I was on to something. That lump felt really, really strange. Just for fun, I refused to let him enter the office complex. He started yelling. People gathered around like they always do, and it was the unanimous decision of the crowd that the man show me what he had in his pocket. Now he couldn't go away without raising their suspicion, and what he had in his pocket was clearly too embarrassing to reveal.

'Empty your pocket!' the crowd began chanting. 'Empty your pocket! Empty your pocket!' The man finally stuck his hand into his pocket and removed a… no, I'll tell you later. That way, you'll hang around longer.

Will you have some tea? 'Aye Chandra!' I shout at one of the waiters running past at breakneck speed. 'Bring two teas!' Their tea is good. At least it keeps me awake. It's so cool and comfortable inside this office complex, I doze off without even knowing it. But those days are gone when security guards could nap on the job. The world has become a dangerous place. At least, that's what they say on TV. Our head of security says no one must be trusted, all unknown visitors are to be frisked, all bags opened, no chances are to be taken.

What do I think of it? Come closer. POOOOOO. Hahaha, that's what I think of people trying to spread panic and paranoia. The times are bad, I won't deny that. But I think it's nobler to die than live with fear and mistrust.

Hang on, here's another man wanting to go in. This is strange. People never enter from this side entrance. Now, since you've come, this is the second visitor. Are you bad luck for everyone? Hahaha, just kidding. Hang on, this guy even has a bag. 'Open your bag,' I tell him. The visitor places his maroon leather bag on the ground and struggles with the zipper. I squat beside him. 'Is it broken?' I ask. He doesn't answer, he seems nervous that the zipper won't open. 'Forget it.' I stand up. 'Go, go in,' I tell the visitor.

Ah, here's the tea. Drink, drink. It's good, isn't it?

No, we never frisk women. Alas, hahaha. I hope I'm around when that day comes. Hahaha, tch, tch, what terrible thoughts. Mrs Pawar would wallop me if she knew. But it's an exciting idea, isn't it? I imagine it all the time. I would make the woman raise her arms. I would press the soft sides of her breasts and then roam my hands down her body to her soft stomach and…

Wait, where are you going? Come back! What else am I supposed to do all day? Hahaha. Wait! It was a bra! The lump in that man's pocket was a balled-up bra! Hahaha… Watch out!

Jyothi

Watch it! Can't you see I'm mopping here?

No! Not from there, it's wet. Go from the left. I'll mop that part of the floor after you've passed.

God knows what world people live in. They seem to be sleepwalking most of the time. They *see* me mopping the floor, they *see* it's wet, and *still* they walk right over it. You're most welcome to leave your footprints—people will revere you and call you Mahatma—but can you please not do so on *this* floor?

Well, it's not your father's floor, some offended men and women shout back at me.

That really steams my idli. Say anything you want, but never go on my mother-father: S.V. Krishnan and O.P. Geetha respectively.

My parents don't know I am a cleaning lady in this office complex. Sitting in our hot, brooding village of Eenamen, they think I am a salesgirl at a saree store in Dubai. I telephone them every Saturday at their neighbour's house. I am sure at least one of them cries or sighs bitterly after hanging up. But my parents would rather have this than anything in the world. Finally, like all other families in the village, they believe they too have a child working in the Middle East.

I did go to Dubai. The agent tried to rape me on the second day. I was about to stab him in self-defence when all that running about the hotel room trying to pin down a stocky woman like me proved too heavy for the agent's heart and he had an attack and died right there. I took my three lakh from his suitcase and flew back to India, to my friend's home in Mumbai. Now I send a little of that money to my parents every month. This cleaning-lady job is enough for my needs.

On the phone I drop hints to my father all the time. 'Appai, I hating Dubai. Appai, I wanting come back to India.' But my poor father pleads with me to stay put. I miss home so much sometimes, I almost want to catch the next bus back to Eenamen. Instead, I yell my lungs out at visitors and employees in this office complex.

WHERE YOU GOING, BLIND BAT! CAN'T SEE I'M MOPPING?

Virat

What's her friggin' problem! Illiterate woman.

Excuse me? Hi. You got a minute? Hi, I'm Virat. I volunteer for an environmental… No, no, I'm not going to lecture you about rainforests or depleting fuel sources. Much as those are pressing issues, I'm going to be more concrete.

Let's discuss this office complex. This place is centrally air-conditioned by a hundred-tonne unit mounted on the top floor. It is pumping countless litres of hydrocarbons into the atmosphere even as we speak. Have you thought about it? Have you thought about how this noxious air will not just disappear, but will travel up, and then around, across the country, dirtying and polluting the air of far-off, innocent people in some far-off, unsuspecting town, where life will get warmer, the summers intolerable, and where an extra bead of sweat on a farmer's pain-creased brow will have *your* karmic imprint on it?

Is this what we want our country to become? An air-conditioned mirage in the middle of a hot desert?

I've spoken to so many people here. They all think I'm off my rocker. Look at the comfort, they say, it's so nice inside this office complex, like a hill station. And how is it outside, I ask. Hot and unbearable, they reply. Exactly, I say, and it's becoming worse outside because of the air conditioning inside. They look at me strangely, and then they ask, you got nothing better to do?

I don't. Honestly.

I have nothing better to do than roam office complexes like these in this SAVEARTH T-shirt, distributing pamphlets to people who don't give a damn about anything more than ten feet and two days away. After college gets over at noon, I could easily go home and light up while surfing for porn, or bring a girl over and mess around while my super-successful parents strut about trying to earn more and more money, much more than we require, not at a physical level, but for our spiritual and inspirational subsistence.

I think I have a Christ-fixation. I want to save—not myself, my parents, or even, to be honest, the environment—I want to save the world. Nothing less than the world. This environmentalism is a starting point. Next, I will work part-time at a rehab centre. And one day I will kick the crutch of external action and meditate on a universal solution that will...

Sorry, coming back to this office complex. Structures like this are a very bad idea, just remember that.

Anil

Uff, thank goodness, he let me go. I thought he would never stop with his lecture. What wrong have I done? Why was he eating *my* brains? I don't own this office complex. I'm just the lift-man on my way to the loo.

Ohh, I really have to go.

What are you doing? No way you're coming in with me! Wait outside.

Aah, what relief.

You're still here?

OK, come along. I'm Anil. I man the elevator in the central lobby. Hurry, walk faster. I've been away too long. Before I came to use the loo and was held up by that sermonizing weirdo, I had gone outside for a cigarette break, which, coupled with a leisurely reading of the day's newspaper and a refreshing discussion with the peanut and newspaper vendors outside the gate, amounted to a good two-hour recess. High time I got back. In half an hour, hordes of hungry office workers from the upper floors will want to come down—they will not take kindly to an unmanned elevator.

Here we are. Welcome to my six-by-eight office. No, no, this stool is for me. You will have to stand in that corner; when someone enters the lift, make an impatient face, so people will think you are actually going somewhere.

Yes, it is always this bright in here. The six tube lights—four too many—coupled with the stainless steel walls and the huge dressing mirror produce an unbearably dazzling, blinding effect. In my faded orange cotton uniform, I feel downright dull in comparison.

STOP	
4	5
2	3
G	1
> <	< >
?	?
FAN	ALARM

This is it. Thirty-two years of my life have amounted to this: pressing ten laminated buttons for three thousand rupees a month.

'Ya, ya, just email the document…'

Ssh, someone's coming. Act impatient.

A man in a suit and tie enters the elevator. I don't know who he is. Must be a visitor or something. I stand up. 'Zip the file. The password is lipika090…' The man is talking on his cell phone. He doesn't notice me.

'What floor, sir?' I ask.

He doesn't hear me. 'Tell him to track his changes to the document…' The man shoots his arm past my face and presses number 4.

The doors close. 'Hello…hello?' the man shouts into his cell phone. 'Fuck, no signal.' The elevator begins its ascent. I stare at the floor numbers flashing in the screen beside the STOP button.

The man brushes his hand past my shoulder to press the fan switch.

He jams his briefcase between his legs and adjusts his tie in the dressing mirror. 2…3… When the elevator slows at the fourth floor, the guy gives a little cough, and when the doors part, he wriggles his shoulders and sweeps out like a man ready to conquer the world.

The elevator returns to the ground floor.

Screw this, I'm going on another cigarette break. If someone asks where I am, tell them I sprained my finger.

From all that button pressing.

Minu Mamdani

Where in God's name is the lift-man? And why is the elevator fan on? What's that scraping noise when the doors open and close? Is a bolt loose? Should I press 3? Should I inspect the third floor? What new horrors await me today?

Has Housekeeping already mopped the third floor? Is that what I think it is? How come no one noticed the puddle of vomit in the corner? Are the Housekeeping staff kidding me?

Isn't that the owner of I&R Ltd? Should I say hello to him? If I say hello, will the other office owners think that I, the manager of this office complex, am partial to the owner of I&R Ltd? Should I just forget about it?

Isn't it lovely in here? Doesn't it feel like you are in Singapore or Hong Kong? When will the whole of India be like this?

Do I smell smoke? Is that man smoking in here? 'You moron? Can't you see the no-smoking sign? Now will you extinguish that thing or should I call security?' Did you see how frightened he was? Did you see how he stubbed the cigarette on his trousers and nearly burnt himself? What a monkey, no? With people like that, how will our country ever shine?

Can you hear the music in the background? Do you know it was my idea to have music piping through the office complex? Why don't you tell me what's playing? '*Hum dil de chuke sanam*'? Are you that backward? Don't you watch films? Haven't you seen '*Aa ab laut chale*'? Isn't this song fabulous? But do you know something? Can you believe there is a man on the second floor who wants us to kill the lobby music? How can this music disturb anyone?

What is this? Whose bag is this? Should I ask that woman? 'Excuse me, miss, is this your bag?' No? Then whose is it? Why has someone left a maroon leather bag under this sofa? Should I check to see what's inside? Could it be drugs? What if it is an explosive? A bomb? Could it be a *bomb*? *Is this the end*?

WHOSE BAG IS THIS!!!

Kishore

'I'm sorry, I'm sorry!' I come running. 'It's my bag!'

'Are you nuts?' the woman screeches. 'Have you gone completely insane? How can you leave your bag around like that? What world do you come from?'

What's with all the questions? Can't she just make a normal statement? And why am I asking so many questions? Is it contagious? 'What's it to you?' There I go again.

'What's it to me?' the woman cries at a dolphin's pitch. 'You know who I am?' She points to the plastic tag on her blazer's lapel. 'You know I can call security and have you thrown out in one second?'

I read the tag: 'Ms Minu Mamdani, Arcade Manager.' That explains it. While she continues to gripe over the bag lying under the sofa, I remove a book from my backpack and present it to her with both hands and a slight bow, like a butler.

'What is this?' the arcade manager says. 'Why are you giving me this book? What am I...' When she glances at the title, her pink mouth blossoms into a megawatt smile. Ah, always the same reaction. She grins coyly and takes the book from my hands.

'I sell these,' I say.

'Salesmen aren't allowed in here, you know,' she says, but I can see she doesn't mean it. She lingers over the contents page; she flips through the book. 'How much?'

'For you, madam? With compliments.'

She giggles. Her lips stretch tightly over her front upper teeth. She runs her hand over the book with hope and a delicate sensuality.

'Please, madam, don't say no.'

She purses her lips. 'OK, thanks. But don't leave your bag around like this again.' Then she walks away with a copy of *Stop Working: The Art of Retiring Now* (MRP Rs 96).

Never mind, one piddling freebie won't ruin me.

I remove forty volumes from the leather bag. Keeping two aside for display purposes, I stuff the rest into my backpack and push the leather bag back under the sofa.

I walk into another office.

'Yes?' a clerk says.

I give him the book. He starts reading it immediately. He extends a hundred-rupee note in my direction and doesn't want to be disturbed with the change. I whiz through the office and manage to sell a copy to each employee at every desk. Even the CEO of the company buys one.

Stop Working: The Art of Retiring Now.

Clearly, a best-seller. I come out of the office with an empty backpack and a waist-pouch full of money. I've already sold 2,000 copies—500 since morning in this office complex alone—and I still have three floors to go. So much better than selling policies.

Oh, myself Kishore, by the way. I used to peddle insurance to residences. That didn't work out, for some reason. I am glad I left that job. Now I am a door-to-door salesman for Sushi Publications. My wife Vinti and I are expecting a child. Two months to go for the delivery. I think the child is going to be lucky for us. It is not yet born and already I am doing so well at work. If I can sell 5,000 copies of this book, if I can somehow manage it, I will book a flat in an under-construction building in Kandivali—a sort of welcome-to-earth present for our newborn from its grateful parents. Pray for us, OK?

I take my leather bag from under the sofa and lug it to the canteen.

I opt for a seat by the window. The waiter wipes the table with a wet rag. I order a plate of rice and daal and drink refreshing cold water from the steel glass. This is the life!

The man at the adjoining table, a late-thirties, fair-skinned, well-dressed type, orders his food. A successful salesman never misses a single chance. I whip out a copy from my bag and extend it coolly in my fellow diner's direction. 'Friend,' I say with my million-dollar smile, 'would you like to read this till your lunch arrives?'

He laughs. He takes the book, flips it over and points to the author's photo on the back cover. 'And I'm still working,' he says.

'Even chefs need to eat,' I say without missing a beat.

'Not their own food.'

'Sometimes that's the best there is…'

He laughs harder and slaps a hundred on my table. 'Keep at it…'

I eat with the satisfaction of being the best salesman in the world.

Nice Water

I have a bad stomach since last night. It is making a gur-gur sound. Now my left arm is paining as well. But I still have to go. My mistresses will want me at work even if my limbs are torn off and I have to crawl on my torso like a caterpillar. To add to my headache, there's no water to bathe with. I took so long doing toilet at the railway tracks this morning that by the time I got in line the taps had gone dry; they will remain so till tomorrow morning. The sixth-floor lady will be quick to say, 'Chhee, you're smelling like a pig!' What to do? Dirty or clean, I must leave for work right away.

Good thing the children are still sleeping. Had they woken up, they would have wanted water to wash their mouths and arses. Seeing no water, all five would've played drums on my head. As if I'm some slave who has to keep everything ready. Chhya! Let them go thirsty or fend for themselves.

I place the lunch box at the bottom of my bag and carefully position the bottle of water on top of it. The water is sparkling like a diamond. I hope the sixth-floor lady lets me keep it in her fridge. It'll be nice to have cold water with lunch. I fix my saree in the mirror. Before leaving for the station, I pause at the door of my two-room hovel to relish the sight of my five children sleeping soundly.

Good, the train is here and so are my friends. We work as servants in a neighbourhood of Byculla. Some of us have served the same houses for twenty-five years: cleaning floors, scrubbing vessels, washing clothes. We go to work together, eat together and come back home together. But I don't like travelling by this Harbour Line; it's always crowded, and the trains are always late.

From the way she is reeking, it seems even Gangu has missed her bath this morning. As we huddle on the floor of the ladies' compartment, I ask, 'Gangu, doesn't your husband launder rich peoples' clothes?' I pinch my nose and continue, 'Then why he doesn't throw you on the pile and whack you clean with his bat?'

Gangu looks at Shanta, Kamala and Sushila; she rolls her eyes at me and says, 'Nanda, shut up, you smelly widow!' We all burst into giggles. My name is Nanda. All of us look the same: small faces, thin bodies, dark skin and big, black teeth.

As our station approaches, I realize the gur-gur in my stomach has stopped. But now I feel weak. Anyway. Work will cure my ills.

As soon as the doors part, I shout, 'Hurry, hurry!' Shanta and I leap together into the lift. The other women work in neighbouring buildings. This lift is so scary; its doors open and close on their own.

'Hey, hey, no jumping here like villagers!' the lift-man says. He presses floors 2 and 6 and moans as his hand brushes against the edge of Shanta's saree: 'Ooh, so soft and silky!'

While walking out on the second floor, Shanta bumps her hip against the seated lift-man's shoulder. 'Bastard, I'll tell my mistress you're troubling me.'

Shanta is from Jalgaon; women from there are all like her:

loud-mouthed and wanton. We Konkanis from the coast are brought up more strictly. No one dare misbehave with me.

This sixth-floor family are fools. They moved into the building a year ago. My mistress's name is Sakkar. She is very old with white hair and a sharp nose. Almost every morning I have to keep on ringing the doorbell before she and her husband rise from their slumber. When it happened the first day, I thought no one was home and went to sit in the garden below. Sakkar told the lift-man to ask me to come up. What a fight we had. She called me a lazy bum who didn't want to work honestly. I told her to clean her ears so she could hear when someone rang their bell.

Sakkar opens her door. 'Chhee! Didn't have bath today? Smelling like a pig!' she says, as I walk past her to the bathroom.

Her husband comes hooting like an owl, 'Who, who? Who's smelling like a pig?'

Sakkar tells him.

The old man asks me with a dirty smile, 'Got up late today, Nanda?'

I slap my forehead and proceed.

As I squat in the bathroom battering their clothes with the washing bat, I notice someone standing behind me. I turn to see. It is the old man staring at my behind. I am not scared. I keep looking at him and whack the bat harder and harder on the clothes. *Bam, bam, bam!* He gets scared and goes away.

Sakkar comes running. 'Aye, you want to tear my clothes or what?'

I giggle and slow down. Sakkar squats outside the bathroom. 'I have some leftovers from last night,' she says, 'rice and mutton curry.' I twist around to answer her. Suddenly, fresh pain shoots up my left arm. I suck air through my teeth.

'What happened?' Sakkar asks.

'I got hit on the arm, paining me very much,' I reply.

'Wait, I'll give you Crocin.' She uses my shoulder as support to get up. Must weigh at least a tonne.

After I hang the clothes to dry and sweep the floor, Sakkar calls me to have tea. I go and squat in the kitchen. She gives me a cup and saucer and a pill. We start talking about the seventh-floor lady, the one whose husband left her.

'Some other woman?' Sakkar asks.

'No, no!' I say. 'He left her to become a sadhu. I saw his bald head when he was leaving.'

'If I were him, even I would leave such a woman,' Sakkar says.

The phone rings in the hall.

'Oh Nanda, it's for you!' the old man shouts.

I drop the cup and saucer and start shrieking.

'What happened!' Sakkar screams.

'Madam, phone has come for me. Oh God, oh!' I sob as tears blur my sight. Sakkar throws a rag on the tea and tells me to at least go see first!

I get up on shivery knees. I clutch my chest and go to the hall. By now I am weeping and howling. Working for twenty years in this building, I have got only one phone call so far—seven years ago, at the third-floor lady's house. My son had telephoned when my husband died from drinking bad liquor. How I cried and cried. Sakkar's husband hands me the receiver.

'Halla?' I say.

'Is that you, Mother?' my eldest son asks. He is twenty-seven and just like his father: doesn't work, drinks all day, now on to his second wife.

'Yes, Ashok, it is me,' I say and start wailing.

'What is it, why are you crying?' my son asks.

'Who? Who died?' I ask him.

The old man rubs my back to comfort me. I shriek more loudly.

'Stop crying, Mother! Why didn't you fill the water today?' my son says.

'What water?' I ask.

'Mother, you stupid, there's no water in the house!' he screams.

'Aye, you worm shit!' I shout back. The old man jerks away his hand. My tears stop. 'Calling me at work for such-such things? If you want water, go to your wife's house! I am not your servant!' I put the phone down. The rascal. His first wife died of jaundice. His second wife lives in her own house and throws him out every night.

Sakkar asks what happened. I tell her. She comforts me with kissing sounds. I bring out the bottle of water from my bag. 'Madam, I can keep this in your fridge for some time?' I ask her as I wipe my tears, thinking she will feel sorry and say yes.

She asks what's in the bottle. Just water, I tell her. 'Oh ho! Now you also want cold water with lunch, is it?' she says. I beg for just a little space in her fridge. 'No need. Wipe the tea, take the leftovers and get lost!'

In the centre are tiffin boxes of rice, newspaper rolls of rotis, paper bundles with scraps of vegetable dishes and a plastic box containing the mutton curry I got from the sixth-floor lady's house. Kamala, Sushila, Shanta, Gangu, Savita and I are sitting in a circle in the society's garden. Lunchtime. We are so tired we are just staring at the food.

'Start, no!' Sushila says.

'You hungry bitch,' Kamala mutters. We all giggle. Shanta tears a roti and dips a piece into the mutton curry. 'Aye, aye, slow down, everyone wants to taste that,' Kamala tells her.

'Your hands are paralysed or what? You also eat if you want,' Shanta replies.

We attack the food and in some time everything is gone. The breeze takes away the newspaper bundles and the remaining mess the crows and dogs will clean off. One by one, we all start burping. I dip my hand in my bag and take out the bottle of water. 'Open it for me, will you,' I say, and hand it to Gangu.

Everyone's eyes widen. 'Where you got this from?' Gangu asks, touching her chin with her fingers.

I sigh and say, 'If you won't open, give it to Sushila.'

Sushila snatches the bottle from Gangu's hand and examines it. 'Oh God, oh, this is pure. Look, look, it's not even been opened!' She says, showing the bottle to Kamala.

'Aye widow, tell, no, where you got this bottle from?' Sushila asks, peeling away the plastic seal.

I snatch back the bottle and twist open the cap. 'From the railway tracks this morning,' I say.

'Agga! Why you went there in the morning? To see all the men doing toilet?' Shanta asks and everyone starts giggling.

'Aye whore, shut up,' I tell her. 'I had to go. I had a bad stomach.'

'So this bottle was just lying there or what?' Shanta asks slyly. I pour the water in my mouth and gulp loudly like a pigeon. 'No,' I say, 'It wasn't just lying there. Some bastard threw it at me from the train.'

'What bastard, which train?' Kamala asks.

'What, so many questions, shee!' I say with irritation. 'I was squatting. A train came and stopped right in front of me. I hid my face with my saree and covered my lower parts with my hands, but someone still threw the bottle to drive me away. It hit my shoulder; good thing the bottle did not burst.'

'Son of a whore! Don't their mothers need to go?' Kamala yells at no one in particular.

Savita begs, 'Please, aye Nanda, give one sip from the bottle, no? Just one sip.' Even Sushila asks for a sip.

'What is this! You beggars will finish my water!' I shout. I put away the bottle and get up to leave.

'Rascal widow,' Sushila mutters to my back and the rest of them giggle.

These donkey women know what I have with me is even more precious than blood.

On my way up to the ninth-floor lady's house, the lift-man smiles at me cheaply. I don't like Shanta, but it is good to have her around at such times. The lift crosses the third floor. The lift-man starts singing, 'What is behind the blouse? What is behind the blouse? What is under the saree? What is under the saree?' I glare at him like the saucer-eyed Khandoba idol in the temple behind my childhood home in Gholvad. My brother still lives there with his fifth wife and seven children.

As soon as Inara, the ninth-floor lady, opens her door she starts, 'I've told you to come earlier, have I not? Now my whole afternoon sleep will be spoiled. I should cut your pay, then you'll know.' First my friends begging for one sip each, then the lift-man singing at me cheaply, and now this. 'You women do such things purposely to harass us rich people. How will you be happy till you don't make others happy?' Inara goes on and on.

I become very angry and say loudly, 'Oka, oka, eenaaf!' Inara is stunned and turns to look at me. I continue, 'I am here now, no? Don't waste my time with your kut-kut. Let me finish the work and be gone.' She keeps staring at me in shock as I start sweeping the hall. I have heard her saying 'Okay-Okay-enough' to her husband when he nags her too much; after that the man falls quiet like a dead parrot.

When I go to sweep the bedroom, I find Inara's two-year-old daughter playing on the floor. I pick up the child and bring her to the hall. The tot clutches my blouse and doesn't let go of it even after I have put her down. I pry open her fingers. She says, 'Num-num, give.' What to do? These rich women stop feeding their children so soon. But the child still misses it. What the child needs, it will ask for. Did my children ever grab strange women's blouses and say 'num-num'? Never. I have fed each of my children to their heart's content.

After I finish sweeping and mopping the bedroom, I clean the kitchen. Then I drag the bucket back to the hall to wipe the floor. There, I see something that spears my heart. I scream, 'You bastard child!' The tot has removed the bottle of water from my bag. She is laughing and splashing the water on the floor like it is nothing. I run to the girl and snatch the bottle. My heart feels as if a butcher's knife is mincing it. The girl begins to cry.

'How dare you call my child a bastard!' Inara comes screaming from the kitchen. She is holding a milk bottle.

I kneel on the floor and start looking for my bottle's cap. 'Your child! Your child was throwing away my water!' I say with tears in my voice.

'For your dirty water you made my kid cry? Get out, you mad woman, you are not fit to work!' Inara yells at me and picks up her daughter.

The child has emptied more than half the bottle. There is a shiny puddle on the floor. I look around for some way to save the spilled water. I cannot let it go to waste. It doesn't smell of the gutter. There are no worms in it. It sparkles like a diamond. For this water, I have borne a blow on the arm and humiliation before a train full of men. This water will not make me feel like I have drunk poison. It will not give me a bad stomach or blotches on the skin. This water will give me life; it will not kill me. I cannot let this water go to waste.

I bring my face down and start licking the water off the floor.

'Shee!' Inara screams, 'Shee, shee, shee! Are you a woman or a dog? Get out of my house. Get out!'

I will not let this water go to waste. Tiny specks of dust and strands of hair come in my mouth. I spit them out. I keep licking the water off the floor till everything is gone. 'Shee, shee, shee! Stop this dirtiness, you dog! Dog!' Inara screams and prods my back with the tips of her fingers.

I get up and say, 'Give my salary.'

The child is still crying. 'I'll give you a slap if you don't get out right now,' Inara shouts, 'I'll pay you at the end of the month. Now go and don't come back!' I put the bottle in my bag and wipe my face with my saree. Through my burning eyes, everything seems watery. Inara pushes me towards the door as if I'm a drunkard, 'Go!'

I spit out a hair and stumble out of her flat.

The Watchman

SOMEONE is going to die today. When I arrive on duty at 7 a.m., I see a cat with blood-smeared whiskers sneaking out of the building gate.

While sipping my morning cup of tea, I spill a drop on the *C* of *SHIV SECURITY* embroidered on my company uniform.

Then the milkman arrives wearing a blue shirt.

I close my eyes. I don't need to see any more. I know what will happen next.

One: a pigeon will come to roost on the gate's lamp post.

Two: the third-floor youth will return from the pool on his motorbike.

Three: the vegetable lady will set up shop on the pavement outside; and nestled in her hair bun will be a single blood-red rose.

Without verifying the sequence of events, with my eyes still closed, I turn around and enter the security cabin.

Pandey, my fellow day-shift watchman, is having breakfast from a tiffin box. He looks up in alarm. 'Who's watching the gate, Mishra?' he asks. Pandey's tone is without rancour. The gate isn't to be left unattended even for a second.

'Someone is going to die today,' I say. I return to my position at the gate. *Let me be wrong.* I stare at the gravel on the ground. *Please?* I look up and around.

No!

There is the pigeon. Parked *there* is the swimmer's bike. And pinned to the just-arrived vegetable lady's hair bun is a maroon, blossoming . . .

Yes. Someone is going to die today, and I can do nothing about it but, just wait to be proved correct.

Pandey takes up position beside me at the gate. We are trained to stand with parted legs, raised necks, and hands locked behind our backs; to not smile like doormats or frown like jailers; to guard with a detached alertness.

STRONG & COURTEOUS. SHIV SECURITY. PROVIDING SOUND SLEEP FOR 21 YEARS.

One would think we were trained for a more profound purpose.

'What… what happened? Tell me,' Pandey says.

From the milkman's blue shirt to the rose in the vegetable lady's bun—I exclude nothing. 'These same things happened the morning Paresh-bhai…' I trail off.

'Are you absolutely sure?' Pandey asks.

'Yes,' I reply. I glance at him. 'Don't look at me that way. You know I'm no seer.'

Pandey mutes the fearful awe in his eyes.

One morning several months ago, around this time, Paresh-bhai, the second-floor resident, had hailed a taxi. Right about then a passing truck burst one of its tyres. The vehicle bucked, skidded across the road, and mowed down Paresh-bhai like a stalk of walking, talking human weed.

That morning, when I heard Paresh-bhai squeal, I was studying the red rose in the vegetable lady's hair. And before that I was watching the third-floor boy park his bike. And just before that I was awed by the pigeon perched precariously on the lamp post. And before that… on and on, identically, unmistakably.

'We must do someth...'

'No!' I cut Pandey off. What could we do? Signs had lined up like the dots children join to complete a picture. I have tried not to look at things. But if a watchman won't watch, what else will he do? I have tried to ignore patterns, only to learn I have no control over the mind—it remembers everything: beautiful or ugly, consequential or not. Some days I dream of working in a mine. I imagine myself chipping off rocks deep underground, where there will be nothing to see and no designs to remember. But today, someone is going to die. And, unfortunately, I know. I know.

'Mishra, what are you doing!' Pandey cries out. I have placed a blob of white lime on my left palm and sprinkled flakes of tobacco on it. Pandey doesn't notice till I begin grinding the mixture with my right thumb.

I roll the paste into a ball and jam it between my lower lip and teeth.

Pandey watches with shock. 'That's too much! You'll be stoned for hours!'

'That's the whole idea,' I say. I want to be out of my mind for hours; hopefully, by then, whoever has to die would have died.

The narcotic blend stuns my mouth.

My salivary glands shut down. White lime slithers across my gums. Tobacco flakes fuse with my teeth. And then...

And then cautiously, little by little, saliva begins trickling in again. Once spit meets lime, the tobacco flakes dance. The uproar of intoxication numbs my senses in seconds.

Now I am only a thing standing by the gate. The person in me won't be back for a while.

The Sunday morning grows busier. People start to go in and out the gate of Sea View Apartments. Pandey begins calling out to residents as they come and go. 'Take care, sir! Take care, madam!'

What a fool. As if you can tell people not to die.

'Mishra!' Pandey nudges me urgently. Through my blurred vision I can sense a huge orange object zooming towards us. Its edges are glinting. When it is almost upon us, I… I raise my trembling hand and salute.

Whew! It was only the seventh-floor resident's Santro on its way out.

Several more false alarms ring through the day. Each time Pandey winces and runs to save some child or woman or man who he fears might be run over by a reversing water tanker or might fall into an open gutter.

By late afternoon, I stop slurring and swaying. 'Welcome back,' Pandey says.

I spit out the narcotic cud. My senses may have cleared, but with clarity comes a physically excruciating sense of dread.

Pandey retreats into the security cabin, this time for lunch. No tobacco, alcohol or drugs for him. Pandey's opiate is food.

Standing alone at the gate, I survey the scene: at eye level, the cemented compound; overhead, the wind-beaten twelve-storey building; outside, the street with non-stop traffic; and people everywhere, all of them oblivious to constantly lurking death.

'Aahhrrrp!' Fifteen minutes later, Pandey announces his return with a loud burp. He bounds up beside me like an excited animal. 'Anyone dies?'

I look at his wide-eyed, eager face. Hadn't he considered the possibility?

'What if it's you?' I ask.

An intense wave of terror passes over his face. And then he says, 'What if it's you?'

I chuckle tiredly.

In five more hours, at 7 p.m., our duty will end.

The wait begins.

2.15.

2.30.

3.

At 3.30, Baadal, the cycle-mounted tea vendor, rides into the gate, veering to the right to balance the can slung on the left side of his cycle.

He jumps off nimbly, rests the cycle against his bony hip, and pours us two cups of tea. Pandey takes his. He refuses to hand me mine. The petty man. Baadal pours a cup for himself. We start slurping at the syrupy brew.

'Someone is going to die today,' Pandey blurts. He glances at me with a vicious triumph.

Baadal continues to drink the tea.

'You heard what I said or no?' Pandey raises his voice. 'I said someone is going to die today!'

'Ya, so? Someone dies every day,' Baadal says. He takes our money, mounts his cycle, and goes away.

'Stupid punk,' Pandey mutters under his breath.

A hot breeze sweeps through the compound of Sea View Apartments. A silence descends upon us. Pandey and I stand side by side without a word. The afternoon's dead heat stills the air. Now every movement around us, even the tiniest of motions, takes on an unbearable gravity. That coin slipping from someone's hands. The downward spiral of that sparrow.

'Ui...' Pandey makes a strange guttural sound. I look at him. He is shortening his neck. Widening his eyes. Ballooning his cheeks.

'What happened?'

Pandey runs to the side of the security cabin. I hear him heave. *Hoowyack!* And then I hear the splash of vomit hitting the tarmac.

Pandey takes a bottle of water from the cabin. He rinses his mouth and clears his nose. When he returns, he looks exhausted, harassed.

'Bad food?'

He doesn't answer. He takes up the guard's position.

'Pandey?'

'You're a bastard,' he says. He doesn't look at me. His throat sounds sore from the heaving. 'We can't do anything. What's the point of knowing something if we can't do anything?'

'Why'd you vomit?'

'I couldn't take it,' he says. He looks at me, then looks away. 'The tension was too much for me.'

Vapours from his vomit reach me. Even I can vomit now.

'I just want this to end, Mishra,' Pandey says. 'I've been waiting since morning. You've spoiled my whole day. Now I just want someone to die. I've had enough.'

4.30.

4.45.

5.

5.10.

5.15.

5.20.

5.21.

5.22.

5.23.

5.23.

5.23.

Pandey sees me tapping my watch. 'What?'

'It stopped!' I shout. I knock on the dial. 'I was just looking at my watch! The second hand suddenly stopped!'

I remove the watch from my wrist. I tap the dial several times. When I press it to my ear, I hear a tomb-like silence.

'Let me see.' Pandey takes the watch. He mimics my motions. He hands it back. 'The second hand is on twenty-three.'

'Very strange,' I say.

I hold the watch at a distance. This old metallic object suddenly seems dangerous, like a treacherous best friend. I throw the watch on the ground. After a moment's hesitation, I bring my heel down on it. Hard. Over and over and over. The dial is destroyed beyond recognition. I kick the heap of junk aside.

'You could have saved the strap,' Pandey says.

He doesn't wear a watch; and now, neither do I. Without time, without hope, terrified and anxious, we stand, feet apart, necks raised and hands locked behind our backs. But Pandey and I forget that we are to neither smile nor frown. Instead, we do both. Smiling, frowning, as we struggle to conceal a knowledge too significant to remain hidden, our faces contort into amused, quizzical grimaces. Like schoolmasters who've shat their pants.

Residents of Sea View Apartments start emerging from the building for their Sunday evening constitutionals. As they walk in and out of the gate, Pandey and I are given odd stares, strange glances, lingering looks. A child points at us and starts to cry. The child's mother looks at Pandey and me. She gasps and hugs her child.

'Act normal,' I whisper to Pandey.

'What? How?'

'Smile. Just smile,' I say. I force my lips into a smile. I glance at Pandey. His grimace gives way to a sad, constipated grin.

Residents form groups of two and three in the compound.

Something is being discussed very seriously. Worse, Pandey and I are being looked at repeatedly.

A man breaks away from the group of residents and approaches the gate. 'Mishra! Pandey!'

'Ji, sir?' I say.

'Haan, sir?' Pandey says.

'What's the problem?' the man demands. 'You two are scaring everyone! Have you seen your faces? What happened? Why do you look so scared?'

I peer at Pandey, hoping he will say something. But he is staring at the ground. As usual, it's all up to me. 'No, no problem, sir. We are just doing duty.'

The man studies my face closely. 'Why are you smiling like that, Mishra?'

Now more residents, fifteen or twenty of them, approach the gate.

'What happened?' a woman asks the man who approached us first.

'I don't know,' the man says. 'These two won't tell. Look at their faces.'

'Mishra, Pandey,' another man says. 'What is the matter? Your faces are pale!'

A woman yells, 'Call up their head office! Their supervisor will make them… Oh my God!'

Pandey's legs have given way. He has collapsed on the ground.

I am jostled aside as the residents rush to nurse Pandey. He is thrashing his head from side to side.

Someone splashes water on his face. Pandey comes to and sits up. A doctor in the group checks his eyes. 'It's OK, he's all right!' the doctor announces.

Pandey nods in agreement.

The residents of Sea View Apartments crowd around Pandey. Now they must have an explanation. 'Don't be afraid, son, tell me what's wrong,' an old woman says.

Pandey starts to weep. He buries his face in his hands to hide his tears. The old woman caresses his head. 'Shh, it's OK, just tell us what's wrong...'

Pandey raises his teary face. He looks at me. He points his finger and shouts, 'Don't ask me, ask him! Ask him!' And then he turns inconsolable.

Nineteen pairs of eyes glare at me. My face starts to twitch.

A man says, 'Mishra!'

'Mishra!' two women shout simultaneously.

Another man says, 'Better say something, Mishra! Tell us what's going on here!'

Pandey shakes his head to warn me. But silence is no longer an option.

'Someone is going to die today,' I say.

The residents issue a collective, 'Haan?'

'This morning a baba was passing outside the gate. He prophesied that today someone from this building is going to die.'

A stunned silence. A dog barks. A bus rumbles by. 'Hmm,' a man interjects. Residents look at each other with raised eyebrows. They don't seem angry any more. Their faces have a pensive expression.

Now I am shaking and dry-heaving like Pandey. I too am weeping. 'I don't want anyone to die,' I say. 'Since morning Pandey and I have been worried, going out of our minds. Who will die? Will that sir die? Will that madam die? Who will die?'

Residents are clucking their tongues and shaking their heads in pity.

The old woman who pacified Pandey now squeezes my chin.

'Mishra beta, it is all destiny. No one can predict death. What is going to happen will happen.'

'No, maa-ji,' I say. 'You are just saying this, but death is the worst thing to happen. No one ever wants to die.'

'I want to!' an old man says. Everyone looks at him and he smiles nervously. 'I mean, not right now, but I'm not afraid of death.'

'See?' The old woman nods and smiles. She expects me to be comforted by what the man said.

I smile back weakly.

What if I told these people the truth? There was no baba-vaba. It's me—I'm the harbinger of bad news, I'm the one who looks at everything and remembers everything and peers too deeply into the vault of reality.

A middle-aged man steps forward and smiles kindly. 'Arrey, brother, death is not something to be afraid of.'

I nod.

'He doesn't seem too convinced,' a young woman points out.

And then, when I thought the day couldn't get stranger, events take a turn for the bizarre. The kind-hearted residents of Sea View Apartments take it upon themselves to convince me of the insignificance of death. First, a show of hands is called for to see who isn't afraid of dying. All nineteen residents gathered around the gate raise their arms.

The old woman nods and smiles at me. 'See?' she says.

I smile back weakly.

The young woman points out that I still don't seem convinced.

Next, all the residents are asked to describe how they would like to die. When they speak, they address me.

'With a bang! *Bam!* I wouldn't even want to know!'

'No, not me, I'd like to know in advance.'

'I want to go in my sleep, like my mother.'

'I want a heart attack.'

'I have cancer, so it's not like I have a choice.'

'Really? What kind?'

'Liver.'

'I want to die on stage.'

'I at work.' So on and so forth, till all the residents have their say.

After the last person describes how he would like to die, everyone looks at me, smiling, nodding encouragingly. The old woman strokes my sideburn. 'See?' she says, 'nothing to be sad about. No one minds dying.'

Unfortunately, the effect these morbid testimonies have on me is contrary to what was intended. Not only does my dread deepen, I now begin doubting the sanity of these men and women. 'I appreciate all this,' I say, 'thank you. I am sorry for spoiling your Sunday evening. I will pray for you all. I will pray for your safety and for a long life for all of you. God willing, no one will die.'

The old woman's face droops and she pulls her hand back. The residents seem irritated.

'Are you bloody stupid or something?' a man standing near me says. His face is flushed.

'N-no, sir,' I stutter. 'I…I just said I will pray that…'

'Oh, shut the hell up!' the man says. 'That's what we're trying to tell you. There's nothing to be afraid of. There's nothing to pray for. It's OK to die.'

I try to smile. 'No, I know, sir. I understand. Nothing to be afraid of. Nothing to pray for. I'm sure no one will die.'

The man clenches his jaw. 'You are *really* pissing me off, pal!' he shouts.

A woman standing beside him pats his shoulder. 'Cool it, na!'

The old woman exhales noisily and shakes her head at me. I look around. Everyone seems disapproving.

I say, 'But why is he getting so angry? I am not saying anything! I am agreeing with him. There is nothing to be afraid of. Nothing to pray for. Anyway, I'm sure no one will die.'

'Unnhh!' The man tugs at his hair. 'Stop saying that! Why are you even saying that? So what if someone dies!'

Now this is too much. 'But I don't want anyone to die!'

'Aaaarrggghh!' the man shouts. He jumps forward and grabs me by the elbow. 'You come! Bloody come with me!'

He starts pulling me and I look around for help. But the others are too stunned to react. The man drags me to the road outside the gate.

Now we are standing on the road, on the very spot where Paresh-bhai was crushed by the truck. Buses, cars, taxis and scooters whiz past just a few feet away from us.

The residents follow us out. All eighteen of them are milling around me and the angry man clutching me by the elbow.

I lose my cool. 'Sir, just let go of my arm. Don't make a scene. You are overreacting. I didn't say anything wrong, OK? Let me get back to duty. I'm sure no one will die.'

'Again?' the man screams. He slaps me hard on my left cheek. And the next moment, letting go of my arm, he dives forward in the path of an oncoming BEST bus.

A balcony door slamming in the wind + Bus 65 passing outside the gate + someone shouting Tunnu + an itch on my left thigh = the arrival of a parcel from abroad.

A cat-fight across the road + a crying child + a woman in a

magenta saree + the eighth floor resident's Palio entering the gate = a stranger trying to trespass into Sea View Apartments.

Children playing in the compound + the sixth-floor resident returning home early + a dog and a bitch fornicating behind a parked car = Baadal veering into the gate, keeling over and spilling his entire can of tea.

A girl in a black miniskirt + three crows perched on the first-floor window + a traffic jam + the sound of laughter = a seismic tremor.

I could go on. I also remember, for instance, the chain of events leading to a brawl on the street, a storm and a pain in my chest. Some days I want to gouge my eyes out and plug my ears with molten lead. Maybe then all this remembering will cease. Or maybe then—and this is what I fear—my mind will latch on to some other dormant sense.

The man who dragged me to the road was merely trying to scare me. After diving forward into the path of an oncoming BEST bus, he jumps back, avoiding the vehicle by a few inches. 'See?' he says. 'Dying is that simple.'

I say nothing. I realize I am dealing with a very disturbed man.

The man dives forward again, this time in front of an oncoming taxi.

'See?' he says again, having avoided the taxi by a millimetre. I nod. 'Now, are you still going to pray that no one should die?' the man asks. I shake my head. 'Good.' He smiles. 'You should never believe what those babas say.'

The other residents break into spontaneous applause. But of course. A working-class, superstitious watchman had been taught a lesson in high-class scepticism. I clap as well.

I follow the residents back to the gate. They disperse. Some return to their homes; some go out for a stroll.

Pandey is standing in the guard position. I go and stand beside him. My cheek is still stinging from the slap.

A few minutes later, Pandey says, 'Sorry, yaar.'

We salute as a Tata Sumo exits the gate. No, no, I am sorry. I should have kept my mouth shut. The problem, I now realize, is in the telling.

A puny, poorly dressed man wants to visit flat 802. Pandey buzzes the flat on the intercom. The visitor is known and permission is granted. The man signs in the register and enters the building.

The residents of Sea View Apartments are luminaries in their own right. There is a millionaire who owns the entire top floor. There is an actress on the sixth floor. And throughout the building is a sprinkling of very wealthy businessmen. Security was lax till a decade ago. But the country was poorer back then. And the residents of Sea View were like their countrymen. As the country grew wealthier, so did these residents. Now their lives are impossible without people like Pandey and me protecting them from people like Pandey and me.

Could I be wrong? Is it possible that someone won't die today?

The way the windows of floors three to six are aglow with a bright red, seeing how the sparrows are chirping and flying around like crazy, and sensing the relief of another sunset, I estimate the time to be about 6.30 p.m.

Our duty ends at seven. I have just half an hour left to be proved right. But what if…

No, I cannot be wrong. Someone is going to die today. But what if…

How can I be wrong! There has to be a reason—some reason for me to remember so many idiotic, inconsequential details: A red rose in the vegetable lady's hair! A pigeon perched on a lamp post!

Someone better die in the next half-hour. I see no reason to continue otherwise. If my memory and mind reveal themselves to be worthless, I might as well drink and drug myself to death.

No, if I can think, and if I can remember random sequences of events from weeks and months ago, there has to be a reason, some reason. Within the next half-hour someone will die; and when that happens, I will remain calm. I will not celebrate. I will not grin knowingly at Pandey. I will keep quiet and go home, content in the knowledge that existence has its own plan, and that, watching and watching day in and out, I have somehow cracked that plan's blueprint.

The telephone in the security cabin rings. Pandey goes in to answer it. After a few seconds he shouts, 'Mishra, take, it's DG saab!' DG is the Shiv Security supervisor for this part of the city. Pandey emerges from the cabin. I go in and pick up the receiver.

'Hello?'

'Haan, Mishra, DG here. Are you tired?'

'What, saab?' I asked.

'Boss, are you tired?'

'Uh, as usual, saab. I've been here since morning.'

'Could you, maybe...' DG says, 'somehow stretch it till tomorrow morning?'

'What!'

'Relax, brother, I'm asking for a favour. Rajkumar cannot come for duty. He has guests from his village. If you can't do it, I'll have to fill in for him. Can you do the night shift with Sohrab?'

'But...'

'Ya, what?' DG snaps.

'Why didn't you ask Pandey?'

'Come on! Pandey just got married a month ago. It's too early for his wife to sleep alone. You know how women are in the beginning.'

'Pandey told you this?'

DG laughs. 'Don't be a nut. We have to understand such things.'

'Tomorrow I will have to do the day shift as well?'

DG says he doesn't know yet, but most probably no. Either way, my overtime pay is assured.

'OK,' I say. 'I'll stay.'

What else? Do I have a choice? It is almost 7 p.m. If I refuse to oblige, DG will have to do the night shift. But I don't care about that. It's almost seven and if I do not do as he says, I will have to go home a broken, hopeless man. I will have to admit that my memory and my mind have no purpose, and that all the events I see and remember amount to zilch.

This morning, after what I saw, I was certain someone was going to die today. Now 'today' has become longer. The half-hour deadline has postponed itself. I thought I had grabbed existence by its horns, but the wilful thing has managed to break loose again, leaving me hanging for another twelve hours.

Pandey is very sorry to hear about my double shift. He tells me to go eat something, to shit, piss, stack up on tobacco and white lime and whatever else will keep me awake through the night. 'Go, go fast,' he says. 'I'll wait till you return.'

I walk out of the gate and cross the road.

Before entering the neighbourhood eatery, I look back for a glimpse of Sea View Apartments. Against the backdrop of a dark blue sky, with the street lights and flat lights glittering, and the traffic zooming up and down the road, the setting seems poised for something momentous, something horrendous. I exhale.

It's going to be a long, long night.

Polo (the mint with the…)

Six thousand rupees: after providing decades of meticulous service, this is the salary I now receive every month.

Five lakh forty thousand rupees: the cost of the surveillance system they installed yesterday to videotape, this day forth, every second my colleague Dhodpode and I will spend at work.

Do the math. You will realize why I didn't feel like coming to work this morning. But I came anyway; the atmosphere at home is no less discouraging.

As the first lot of hundred-rupee notes were issued from the minting machine, and as six sample notes fell into each of our slots, Dhodpode and I automatically looked up at the new camera attached to the ceiling.

It has had different effects on us.

The camera has made Dhodpode self-conscious. He is plain-looking like me, with lank hair and a nondescript face sprinkled with tiny boils that we seemed to have inherited from our ancestors. Under the electronic gaze, Dhodpode's movements have become awkward—at times he handles notes with an extra flourish, and at other times it seems his limbs are made of lead. The camera has angered him too. While we were in line to sign the roster this morning, Dhodpode said he was up till late last night, dividing and redividing our salaries against the cost of the new system. It was criminally unfair, no matter how one computed it.

Dhodpode earns as much as I do.

The camera has neither enraged nor embarrassed me. I have no anxieties about my appearance. But it has humiliated me. I thought people considered me to be trustworthy.

Dhodpode and I are sample checking officers; we inspect newly minted currency notes. I don't see why we are needed. The entire process is Italian and automated. We have never detected any flaws. The watermarks, insignias and serial numbers are always where they should be. The police guards, who used to oversee us without making us feel watched, have been replaced by a camera. I wonder why they don't replace both of us as well.

Our humanity, at least for now, must probably be indispensable.

By noon, Dhodpode and I have inspected samples from lots of fifty-, 100- and 500-rupee notes. Here, money is made every day, crores of it; this country seems to be devouring it. If only paper could feed stomachs.

During lunch, Dhodpode took me along to meet the supervisor. I told him nothing would come of it. And nothing did. The supervisor said we worked for the Currency Press of the Government of India. How could they trust anyone with the country's money? So what if we had been inspecting notes for years. So what if policemen had watched over us at all times. The camera was a necessity, now that the government could afford it.

'Had you increased our salaries instead of hanging that, that thing over our heads, you would have earned our loyalty forever,' Dhodpode said.

The supervisor lost his cool. 'This is a modern republic, not some fiefdom that needs your loyalty! In China, they install cameras on the streets. And you, do you realize the gravity of what you do here? The camera is here to stay; just get used to it.'

Dhodpode and I lunched in silence.

When we returned from the canteen, samples from a fresh lot of twenty-rupee notes were waiting to be inspected.

It is by no means easy to enter or leave the room we work in; there are elaborate procedures to fulfil on our way in and a frisking to be undergone on our way out. I don't mention these processes because they are mere technicalities, like punching time cards or signing rosters. But when you consider these technicalities, and when you see how impossible it is to steal a sample note, that camera up there stings like an unjustified aspersion.

'Forty-five months,' Dhodpode said. He was bent over a twenty-rupee note like a jeweller. 'Had they doubled our salaries, that's how long it would have taken them to spend five lakh forty thousand. I could have moved to a closer suburb. I could have got Shruti braces.' (Shruti was his fifteen-year-old daughter.)

'Had they doubled my salary…' I began. But I ran out of words. 'I don't know what I would have done. Probably got new dentures made for my sister… from Shruti's dentist.'

'But now there won't be any damn dentist!' Dhodpode said.

And my ageing, unmarried sister probably doesn't need new dentures either. I don't know anyone else who needs my money. I could, if I tried, find hundreds of people in need of assistance, but charity towards strangers has a desperate ring to it.

During tea break in the canteen, we learnt that we were being relayed live to the Control Room. 'I noticed you both on the mini-TV,' said Bashir, the policeman who used to watch over us in the mornings. 'I thought, arrey, here are Sawant and his partner! I watched you guys for some time, then I got bored.' It was Bashir who told us how much the new system cost.

Dhodpode nearly choked on his tea. 'Who else watches us?' he asked in a high-pitched tone.

'I don't know,' Bashir replied. 'I guess, whoever wants to can just stand and watch you two on the screen.'

Fantastic, I thought.

This new information virtually froze Dhodpode. When we returned, he just sat staring at the samples in his slot. 'Forget about it, act like it's not there,' I urged. He blinked, but he refused to look up or acknowledge me. 'You can talk, you know. They can only see us, they can't hear us,' I said.

Dhodpode looked at me. His eyes strayed to the camera; he quickly looked away as if it were a naked woman one wants, yet hesitates to look at.

At 5.25 p.m., the sample collector arrived to tally records and collect all the samples we had inspected through the day. Dhodpode lingered—just a little—while handing over the 500-rupee notes.

The collector didn't notice. I did.

Sure enough, on our way to the station, Dhodpode set his gaze on something distant and said, 'I wish we didn't have to return everything every evening. Imagine if we could keep something back.'

I have heard previous colleagues say such things.

I looked at Dhodpode, but he seemed lost.

I went home praying he would never get caught.

Mischief in Neta Nagar

THEY say this is a democracy. Full freedom. Do what you want. Live, piss, eat, sleep wherever you wish.

It is 9.30 a.m. If I were a regular guy, I'd be leaving for work. Instead, I am at home, in the loft of my twenty-by-twenty shack on the outskirts of the world's largest slum in the world's soon-to-be most populous city. I am watching TV. Below the loft is the living room where members of my family—my wife and our five children—are eating breakfast. I am in no mood to descend from the loft. I am in bed. I have been watching a cricket match since four in the morning. India vs Pakistan. The second innings is on. Pakistan is batting. The Indian team scored OK. The Pakistanis seem set to win. I want this match to never end. I don't care who wins. India. Pakistan. I don't care. Till the match lasts, I don't want to think about anything else.

Our slum gets free electricity. In exchange, we have to vote en masse for a particular politician. Thanks to this slum, the politician has had a seat in the legislative assembly for ten years in a row. Our slum also gets free water and free phone connections and none of us have to pay rent ever. To feed and clothe my family, I borrow money on zero interest from a bank owned by the aforementioned politician. We call this Neta Nagar. The Politician's Settlement. Neat, ya?

A Pakistani cricketer just got out. Clean bowled. One half of the crowd at Sydney is ecstatic. I am the calm sort. As I said, I don't really care who wins. Three wickets left. Fifty-five runs to be made in sixty balls. Pakistan will win.

My fourth-born, a son, seven years old, comes up to the loft with a slice of fried bread and a cup of tea. He places the tray at the foot of the bed on which my wife and I sleep, and where we spawned all five of our litter. The loft is a bed, that's all it is; there is no room to stand around. The boy sits on the edge of the bed and starts watching the match on the TV set that I have placed near my feet. 'Tanvir!' his mother calls out from below. My son hurries down. Tanvir, yes, that's his name. Sultana, Jumaina, Nadia, Tanvir and Bashir. There will probably be two or three more of them. The politician will never be short of votes as long as I can help it.

Seven runs. Three balls. The commentators are insisting this is a nail-biting end to an exciting match. All I'm worried about is how to spend the rest of the day once the game is over. In my part of the city, this is a constant worry. Having sold our suffrage, we are left to suffer the spoils. If I didn't have television, the idleness would drive me nuts. Sick thoughts come to mind if I sit around doing nothing. I imagine murdering men and women, shooting animals, spying on my neighbour's wife as she bathes…

A boundary. Four runs. Pakistan wins. India loses. Half the crowd cheers. I wash down the slice of oily bread with lukewarm tea. I turn off the television. I crawl to the foot of the bed, wrap my lungi around my waist, and climb down from the loft.

The family watches my descent. My wife resents me. Which wife doesn't resent her husband? Mine grudges my lack of ambition, my non-existent drive. She would like me to work somewhere, like a handful of other men in this slum do, to supplement the freebies from the politician, so we can save the extra cash for the time when the politician no longer cares for us. Do I intend to live in this slum all my life, my wife demands to know.

'I'm outside,' I say. I put on my slippers and step out of our shack. Where should I work? What should I do? And more importantly, why?

I sit on a chair outside the door. I am being alternately roasted by the morning sun and fanned by the cool breeze. I bring out a packet of beedis, light one, and breathe in the acrid fumes. When I close my eyes, snatches from the cricket match flood my mind. India lost. As usual. Try as I might, I cannot find it in me to say 'we lost'. To belong to the community, to the land or the nation, a man must first be in possession of himself. In this slum, each and every one of us is owned. Don't think I am complaining. May the politician live a long life.

Mischief. I am in the mood for mischief.

'Aye!' I shout into my house. 'Aye!'

One of my daughters emerges. She scowls like her mother.

'Bring me the crackers we bought for Eid,' I say.

'They are over,' my daughter informs me with an offensive finality.

I threaten to strike her. She runs into the house.

Her mother emerges. 'What do you want now?' she asks.

'The crackers I bought for Eid.'

'What do you want to do with crackers?' my wife asks.

'Just shut your trap and bring them!'

She goes in. I titter in anticipation of what I am going to do.

My wife emerges five minutes later. 'Take, here.' She throws a loom of crackers in my lap.

The cheek!

I grab her wrist. She tries to free herself. I pull her back. 'Come here, you bloody! Come here!'

'What do you *want*?'

I hold up the crackers. 'Light them,' I say.

'Ya Allah, what kind of man…'

'Shut up!' I shout. I thrust the loom and matchbox into her hands. 'Go on, light them!'

My wife shakes her head in disgust. 'I hope you die!' she says. She jerks my hand off. She walks about fifteen feet from where I am seated. She throws the crackers on the ground. She crouches, lights a match, sets the loom on fire and runs for her life.

I sit up in my seat. I am smiling. The white gunpowdered paper smokes for a second or so. And then it starts sparking.

I get up and slip into my shack and shut the door. My wife and kids look up in confusion.

I watch through a slit in the window. The sparks get closer to the crackers. And then, one by one, the crackers begin to go off.

Phataak! Boom! Phaat! Phataak! Boom!

I start giggling. In a country still mourning its loss of face in a far-off land, these will be the only explosions of celebration, and they will not go unpunished. I wonder where the retribution will come from. The neighbouring Shiv Sena branch? Or the adjoining Dalit-ridden Mangal Nagar? Our patron politician will have to bend backwards to save his Neta Nagar from turning into a battleground.

Worried faces poke out of next-door shacks. I continue to smoke my beedi while contemplating the scene from the slit in my window.

India lost. Pakistan won.

Democracy, no?

Phataak! Boom!

The Thirteenth Floor

In the end, our building's thirteenth floor goes to an American company. The floor's flats are turned into serviced apartments for Rafell Inc.'s expat workforce. It is a direct deal with the builder. None of us earn any commission. In the vacant space where our kids once played carom and table tennis, where our drivers and servants took afternoon naps and where our youngsters held Saturday-night dance parties, now people with names like Brenda and Wesley sleep, eat and watch television. The watchmen claim the Americans are up all night sometimes. Maybe it is the differing time zones and residual jet lag that causes their insomnia. It is more likely, however, that the walls of their thirteenth-floor flat have retained memories of our laughter, our screams, our amorous whispers and stifled sobs, making the air crackle with the excitement and anticipation that we had come to associate with that no-man's-land.

For the first eleven months of Varsh Tower's occupation, the building's thirteenth floor had remained unsold and derelict. We were to blame. We were bankers, businessmen, advertising professionals, doctors, lawyers… Despite being active contributors to the machinery of a so-called modern economy, we nursed the most ludicrous superstitions with regard to colours, numbers and the north–south orientation of beds and kitchens. When it came to booking a flat in Varsh Tower, we, the building's future tenants, were adamant in our choice: anything but the thirteenth floor.

The builder dangled free flat-screen TVs and modular kitchens as bribes. He offered to renumber the building's storeys, skipping thirteen in the count from G to 25. We didn't fall for it. Thirteen by any other name would still retain its malevolent potency.

And so, for the first eleven months of Varsh Tower's occupation, the thirteenth floor sat vacant and unfinished, like the last remaining bachelor from a brood of married siblings. It had holes for windows and no electrical or sanitary fittings. When strangers saw our building from a distance, especially at night, the dark, unoccupied thirteenth floor must have seemed to them like a slice of menace wedged between the twelve cheerfully luminous storeys both above and below it.

The tenants of floors fourteen and above were the first to discover the thirteenth's dark allure. What drew us to it was its unclaimed wilderness. It was no one's. During our initial weeks in Varsh Tower, if the elevator accidentally stopped at the thirteenth floor, the metal doors would open on to a staggering expanse of raw space: windswept and sunny in the day, pitch black and foreboding in the night. Viewing the thirteenth floor was like stepping into the past, it was like witnessing the gray rough-edged birth of our gleaming twenty-five-storey building.

We didn't like what we saw. The thirteenth's un-tiled floor, its exposed cement ceiling and the random-seeming positions of its load-bearing walls made us doubt the specialized expertise that had ordained the dimensions of our own vaastu-friendly homes. Was this the disarray that lay beneath our marble tiles and behind our velvet-finish walls?

Like property owners throughout the island city, we too had

paid too much for our flats in Varsh Tower. Many of us had signed away the greater part of our income for decades to come in order to pay back loans on our homes. It was a monumental act of faith in our future selves. With those home loans, we had forever relinquished the freedom to be whimsical or wayward, reconciling ourselves to lives of chronically overworked members of a society deep in the red. The thirteenth floor was threatening to unsettle our resolve. When we peered into its unoccupied expanse, we saw—well, we saw a great business opportunity. The space was worth crores of rupees. If we could swing the deal for the builder, the earnings from one per cent or two in brokerage would take years off our debt. It would mean we could work less, be less anxious about our jobs, refuse to take on more clients, stay home some more and for once enjoy the flats that we were killing ourselves to finance.

Each of us approached the builder—delicately and on the sly—to offer our help in disposing of the thirteenth floor's unsold flats. It may not have been propitious enough to live in, but we had no objections to earning fat commissions off that inauspicious storey.

The builder, a battered old dog of a man, played us like a coquette, feigning astonishment at our phone calls and over our surreptitious visits to his office. 'Arrey, programmer saab, since when have you entered real estate?' 'Arrey, doctor saab, you're into real estate too?' He would say real estate like it was RDX or opium, making us squirm in our seats.

The thirteenth floor's failure to sell had wounded the builder's pride. It had bled him financially. People like us were to blame. And now, if people like us wished to make money off it, here were the conditions: The entire floor would have to sell en bloc; builder saab wasn't interested in any piecemeal transactions. The payment would have to be made lump sum, in all white, before possession. And there was to be absolutely no negotiation on the price. The effect was akin to being boxed on the head when the builder quoted the figure in crores. Our ears hummed. He wanted almost twice the market value prevailing for a property the size of the thirteenth floor. It was an impossible demand. He knew it. 'I am in no hurry. None whatsoever. My family won't starve if that floor doesn't sell. Let it sit forever. Maybe I'll turn it into a clubhouse or community centre. No hurry at all.'

We came home feeling tinier than cockroaches. Our futures never weighed heavier on us.

Over the coming years each of us would make a variety of attempts to augment our fixed incomes. We would dabble in shares, rent out extra rooms to paying guests and conduct coaching classes for neighbourhood students. Despite our apprehensions, we would manage to get along fine—paying off our EMIs on time while adequately meeting our households' increasing expenses. But the sting of that initial failure in selling Varsh Tower's thirteenth floor would forever colour our perception of wealth and the wealthy. Even when we would become fairly well off ourselves, we would forever guard our faces against the smugness that had crept on to the builder's visage when he said he was in no hurry, when he said he could wait forever. We would hope we never amassed so much as to believe in the eternity of our affluence. But that was in the future…

Meanwhile, some of us made perfunctory efforts to peddle Varsh Tower's thirteenth floor. We advertised the property in newspapers for a few weeks at our expense. Nothing came of it, of course. Inquiry calls would end in laughter when people heard the price we were quoting for the space. 'For the thirteenth floor, that too? You must be joking!' We found it impossible to argue.

Once it was clear that there was no money to be made off it, we lost interest in the thirteenth floor. Now it was just a vacant property where our children hung out, where our wives conducted yoga sessions, where our teenagers partied, and where on Sunday afternoons, our elders held their laughter club meetings. We wondered how they could endure the thirteenth's unpaved floor, its unpainted walls and the lack of electricity and toilet amenities. In bitter moods, we would taunt our families to go live there, given the inordinate amount of time they spent in that wilderness. At least then we wouldn't have to earn so much for the upkeep of our swanky apartments.

Over time, we pinned our hopes on other sources of side income. We ceased to associate the thirteenth floor with the builder's arrogance. We ceased to be annoyed when our families were always itching to go there. In fact, we even began to venture there ourselves.

Half the contents of our homes had landed up in that empty storey. Our cracked coffee tables, wobbly chairs, and the table-tennis table we had no room for in our own flat, the extension wires and old carpets and myriad other things that we thought had been discarded due to lack of space had all converged on the thirteenth floor. Looking out through the windowless holes in the walls made us dizzy. Putting up with the thirteenth's imperfections was a thrill unto itself. And there were the unfinished walls defaced with copious creatively obscene graffiti:

Jiya cucks sock.

Hoof arted ice melted.

Bugi digs Rishi.

Lord is cumming.

Like our families, we too fell for the thirteenth floor.

On a Saturday afternoon, a group of four Americans came

to inspect it, accompanied by the builder's assistant. We and our families were neck-deep in a carom tournament comprising seven boards, twenty-eight players, and twice as many onlookers. By then, we had become regular participants in the thirteenth floor's revelries.

'They got a liddle pardy goin' on here!' commented one of the Americans, a middle-aged white man in a black T-shirt.

'Not to worry, sir,' the builder's assistant assured him. 'All this will be cleared out as soon as you say yes.'

'Yes!' the American said. 'We say yes. The place is close to the airport, close to our office, looks good to me.'

His colleagues seemed surprised. A man of Chinese descent spoke up. 'Josh, come on, you want us to live on the thirteenth?'

The American in the T-shirt shrugged his shoulders. 'We got a deal,' he said to the builder's man, and then, turning to his colleague, 'You believe in crap like that?'

About Your Cell Phone

HELLO! I am the man who stole your cell phone last Monday.

Remember that medical store you entered at Nagpada Junction? I was standing by the counter, waiting to catch the salesman's attention. You strode into the shop as if you owned the place. You demanded condoms with such frankness, in such a loud voice, I immediately decided that you needed to be taught a lesson for the entitlement that life had bestowed upon you.

You placed your helmet on the glass countertop. Then you plonked your cell phone beside it while you commanded the abashed salesman to just hand you the whole damn condom carton so you could choose the brand and size you wanted.

I was surprised by the glitziness of your phone. It was almost too compact and slick for a man of your build and confidence. I tapped my fingers as I inched my hand towards your carelessly placed gizmo. Your pot-like helmet prevented you from spotting the movement of my arm. While you were still torn between ribbed and dotted, I swooped away your phone and slunk out of the shop.

I walked down Clare Road and took a right at Shepherd Road. I took another right towards JJ Bridge and wound my way back to Nagpada Junction. I tried to look for you as I passed by the medical store. You were nowhere in sight.

I began ambling through Madan Pura. You called your phone just as I was passing by Memon Masjid. I admit I was startled by the unexpected loudness of your ring tone. And that annoying music! All those chimes and drums building towards a kitschy, idiotic crescendo. How could you tolerate taking calls after that horror of a soundtrack!

You were beside yourself when I answered. Blowing hot and cold. You cursed me one second, and the next moment you were begging me to return your phone. Was I right to believe that you were almost on the verge of tears? I said nothing. I was too busy figuring you out. Such desperation to retrieve a mere cell phone? You called me a mother-fucking mother-fucker son of a donkey bitch. 'Boss, please,' you begged, 'I'm falling at your feet, just give me back my mobile!'

'Suck my dick,' I said and disconnected the line.

I sat down under the awning of Light of India restaurant. It was late in the afternoon. Neighbourhood schools had begun releasing their underaged inmates for the day. I watched puny, unkempt kids weighed down by gigantic school bags winding their way through Madan Pura's perpetual crush of hawkers, pedestrians, motorcycles, cars and the occasional BEST bus marooned amid it all like a red whale.

Your phone rang several times over the next few minutes. The caller ID showed unknown numbers. I rejected the calls. I knew it was you calling from payphones. I knew you wanted to negotiate a price with me. I silenced your phone's ringer.

'Thambi!' I called out to a waiter from Light of India and ordered a glass of cutting, that far-from-tea bubbling away on Mumbai's footpaths all day and night—sweet and cheap, imbibed and forgotten. Your phone's screen kept flashing mutely to indicate incoming calls and messages and more calls. I slipped the phone into my shirt pocket. I didn't know what to do next. Your phone was the first thing I'd ever flicked in my life.

There was a discomforting buzzing on my right thigh. I brought out my own phone from my trouser pocket. It was thrice your phone's size and weight, and possibly one-tenth the price. *Home* was calling. Panic gripped my heart. I accepted the call. My mother hollered, 'What's taking you so long? The child can't wait any longer!' I could hear my year-old daughter yelling her head off. I'd come out to buy milk powder from the medical store.

A waiter placed a minuscule glass of tea beside me. 'Tea, five rupees.'

'Tea? You stopped to have tea?' my mother hollered some more. 'Here your child is starving without milk and there you're having a gala time!'

There were other things my child was starving for. The love of her mother, for instance.

'I'm coming soon…' I said. My daughter's voice had cracked in exhaustion. Her screeching sounded like a windy whine.

'Oh, this poor, unlucky child…' my mother began. I disconnected her call.

The tea was sickeningly milky and painfully sweet. Among the numerous pejoratives that others would like to use for me—good-for-nothing, wife-beater, idler, slob—here was one more: cell phone thief.

I bought a tin of Nan 1 from another medical store and rushed home.

My mother was doing her evening prayers on the floor. The baby was asleep on a mat next to her. While her lips kept moving and her body performed the motions of the namaz, my mother's furious eyes followed me around my one-room-kitchen flat. I lay down on the cot in the kitchen.

It was hot enough to melt the hair on one's skin. The churning of the ceiling fan made things worse.

Ignoring me, my mother hurried into the kitchen to prepare a milk bottle.

She rushed back to the hall. My daughter let out a wail. And then there was the heavy silence of a deep hunger being finally quenched.

I brought out your phone. Its silver-gold gloss and futuristic design looked out of place in my shabby, overstocked hole of a home.

Your phone's screen was layered with multiple messages indicating missed calls and unopened texts. I began sifting through them. Among the seventeen missed calls, eleven were from someone named Deepika, the last call being just three minutes ago. Deepika had also sent all five text messages.

Plz, this my hubby fon, plz return, v wil reward!!!

Plz giv bak fon v wil giv n e thing u wnt.

Plz whoevr found this fon v wil not b angry plz retrn, big rewrd!!

It had been over an hour since I'd stolen your phone. Had you told your wife where you were at the time? Were those condoms for Deepika, or were they for some other woman, a mistress whom you intended to meet up with for an evening fuck on your way home?

As I looked down at your phone, propped up on my crotch like a digital dick, the screen lit up to indicate yet another incoming call. I panicked for a split second, and then I calmed down when I remembered that I'd put the ringer on silent. Even a split second of an unusual sound would have caught my mother's attention. And then there would be the slew of questions. *What was that noise? I heard some noise. Is it a phone? I heard a phone. Show me your pockets, what are you hiding? Whose phone is this? You stole someone's phone? You thief!*

Someone named Krish J was calling you. I pressed the Accept Call button and raised your phone to my left ear.

There was the drone of passing traffic and the silence of someone awaiting a response. I had no intention of speaking. Ten seconds passed. Krish J finally snapped. 'Hello?' he said. 'You there?'

My stomach quivered. For a second there, it seemed like he knew it wasn't you who had answered the phone. And then this person named Krish J spoke your name. 'Hello, Rishad? Dude, you there?'

Rishad, huh? I'd imagined you to be more of a Rohit or a Prakash, some sinewy small-town north Indian name hinting at a childhood spent in cold winters and scorching summers and a clerk for a father, whose incurable naivety had driven you to be his exact opposite—a bold-faced, bike-riding city dude who broadcasts the activeness of his sex life by making loud demands for condoms from hapless salesmen. But Rishad? Rishad suggested parents who'd taken the trouble to find an unusual name for their son. Maybe they were intellectuals of some sort. How the progeny of such people had turned out to be a pumped-up jock was hard to understand. Rishad just didn't add up with what I'd seen of you at the medical store.

I disconnected the call and slipped your phone under my pillow. My mother had entered the kitchen with my year-old daughter hooked to her waist. 'I have to leave for the majlis,' she said, 'I'll go home to feed your father. I'll be back by ten.' My parents lived in their own one-room-kitchen two streets away. Between them, me, my four siblings and our extended family of cousins and uncles and aunts, our clan held a sizeable chunk of south Mumbai's one-room-kitchen units. I was born and brought up in a one-room-kitchen; I'd never lived in anything bigger than 275 square feet. It's the reason none of us could think of selling up our holes in downtown ghettos and shifting to the suburbs: we would feel marooned in larger flats.

The prospect of spending an evening alone with my infant daughter took the wind out of me. I had no choice. My mother's interminable majlises, salaams, tasbihs and Bibi Fatimah's *thaalees,* all these arcane religious get-togethers performed in the company of a reliable set of female relatives and acquaintances, provided these women with a periodic nourishment of their identities. When my mother returned from one of these services, smelling of attar and incense and belching up fumes of the heavy mohallah food, she would seem reassured of her pious, prudent and clued-in Muslim womanhood.

Gulshan began to wail as my mother deposited her in my lap. She clutched an edge of my mother's muslin dupatta. I had to pry open her tiny fingers. My mother considered Gulshan, her eighth grandchild, the unluckiest among all her grandkids, and me, her fourth-born, her most misfortunate offspring. It's ironic how one woman's decision to seek out her own good life could leave such misery in its wake. My mother cursed my wife fifty times a day. But there was no bringing Dilshad back. She now worked as a production assistant for Hindi films and lived in a Seven Bungalows rental with two other girls. When *Wohi Toh* releases a month from now, I will have to suppress the urge to buy a ticket, sit through the whole film, and scan the end credits for 'Dilshad Nathani'.

After fussing about in the hall, gathering her things and settling the inadvertent paraphernalia of tending to an infant, my mother called out from the door, 'I'm going! Give her a bottle in two hours!' I couldn't see my mother, but I could imagine the look on her pinched face, her manifest annoyance at having to come back to my home, to mend the mess she hadn't created.

'See you, dadi,' I said squeakily, bidding her goodbye on behalf of my daughter.

My home felt bigger with my mother gone. I reclaimed the space. I placed Gulshan on the mat in the hall and got her busy with my phone. I looked out of the window to reclaim the view as well. The tree between our window and the adjoining building provided a green screen of privacy that had allowed Dilshad to roam around our flat in a tank top with no bra and no panties under her rayon pajamas. Those were days of perpetual hard-ons and spontaneous sex, and evenings spent in malls, trying on all the clothes that neither of us could afford. Our paradise ended with the birth of Gulshan. Dilshad became terrified of her body's capacity for seriousness, for procreation, and she became horrified by my obliviousness to the immensity of the looming responsibility.

I checked to see the condition of your phone's screen. Krish J had called a couple of times more. And Deepika was still at it, bombarding your phone with messages begging for it to be returned.

I extricated my phone from Gulshan's hands and replaced it with the TV remote. I needed a number. I'd known it by heart for seven years, but now, in a matter of months, several of the digits had become jumbled in my mind. I scrolled down my Contacts list to S. Shad. That's how I'd christened her on my phone.

I punched in Dilshad's number on your phone's keypad. She had stopped taking calls from my mobile. She had even stopped taking calls from payphones in the area—she'd learned to recognize the area code. I gazed at the familiar sequence of digits on your phone's screen. Dilshad's number. I expected nothing from this call. No indication of a sudden change of heart. No kindness or apology or so much as a query about our daughter, for whom Dilshad claimed she was amassing a sizeable bank balance.

I pressed your phone's Call button.

The unexpected happened. Your phone identified the number I'd dialled. Dilshad's number vanished and this appeared on your phone's screen: *Calling... Jaswant Plumber.* I disconnected the call.

Gulshan had begun crawling around on the floor, venturing into places that were usually out of bounds when my mother was around. I kept an eye on her while re-entering Dilshad's number on your phone. I double-checked the digits and their sequence. I pressed the Call button and once again the same thing: *Calling... Jaswant Plumber.*

I disconnected the call and rushed to extricate Gulshan from under the coffee table. She screamed to be left alone. I brought her back to the mat and handed her the remote once again. I kept the toilet door open as I took a leak. The release of urine focused my mind. Dilshad's number was saved under *Jaswant Plumber* on your phone.

I returned to the hall and picked up Gulshan. Your phone was lying on the divan, its screen glowing to indicate an incoming call. I ventured closer and bent down to have a look. But of course. Jaswant Plumber was calling, possibly in response to my two calls, one of which must have gone through before I could disconnect.

My daughter was pulling on my ear lobe and gurgling to herself. My heart was thumping like the bass in cheap sound systems. I picked up your phone. Jaswant Plumber was still awaiting an answer. 'Pamamaaa…dadama…' Gulshan babbled. I pressed the Call Accept button.

'Rishad saab, where are you? I've been waiting since three!'

It was her! Your Jaswant Plumber was my Shad, my Dilshad! I disconnected the call and flung your phone on the floor mat.

What the fuck, man! Who are you? Why do you have my estranged wife's number saved on your phone under Jaswant Plumber? And why the behenchod hell had she been waiting for you since three? The condoms, were they for…? It was too terrible to conceive.

I put Gulshan down and dialled my mother's cell.

She answered with a nasty whisper. 'What?' I could hear a gang of women chanting a tasbih in the background.

'You have to come back right now,' I said.

My mother whispered some more.

'I don't understand what you're saying. Just come back right now, ma! You have to look after Gulshan. I have to go somewhere urgently.'

The chanting receded, and after much shuffling and closing of doors, my mother finally spoke at top volume. 'Curses on you, Siraj. Disturbing my prayers. I am praying for you, you good-for-nothing ungrateful bum!'

I ignored her diatribe. 'Just come back right now. If you're not here in fifteen minutes, I will have to leave Gulshan with Naju aunty.' My seventy-year-old, half-blind and completely mad neighbour who thought it acceptable to give neighbours leftover food—often two or three days old—'just to taste'.

I switched on the television and played with Gulshan absent-mindedly. Your phone was in my pocket. I didn't need to look at it any more. The time for juvenile snooping was over. This was the first time in my life that I had become aware of a terrifyingly awesome, larger purpose at play. It isn't everyday that a man goes out to buy infant formula and comes back with a smoking gun that might help solve the mystery of his fucked-up, dismal life. Since Dilshad had left home three months ago, I hadn't stopped wondering about her true motives for abandoning me and Gulshan. Now it seemed I might be about to find out.

My mother arrived in ten minutes. She stormed in with the bitterness of a harried harridan. I kissed Gulshan on her little head. If I'd known then that I wasn't going to come back for months, I would never have left.

'I'll see you,' I said to my mother. I put on my slippers and walked out. There was a tremble in the pit of my stomach. How abruptly an ordinary day can turn into one of reckoning.

I stood under my building's awning and sent out two text messages from your phone. One to Deepika: *Pik up phone from Crosswrd bookshop @ Wadala mall at 7.30. I wil b carrying blu backpak.* And another text message to Jaswant Plumber: *Big problem, meet me @ Crosswrd bookshop at Wadala mall, 7.30.* I was shooting in the dark.

You replied from Deepika's number: *Ok i wil b ther.*

Jaswant Plumber's reply, which also came immediately, was the clincher: *Hope all ok baby, ok c u @ 7.30.*

Jaswant Plumber and her baby had a big surprise in store for them.

I rushed off in a taxi to Mahatarpakhadi, to Jignesh's warehouse.

The gun felt heavy for something of such diminutive dimensions. Its weight inspired confidence, otherwise I might have thought Jignesh was lending me a toy. Jignesh Medh, my schoolmate. After standard twelve, everyone I knew had applied for student or tourist visas to America. The lucky ones had been blessed with upright, prosperous lives in Chicago, in Houston, in Atlanta. And the rest of us, the embassy rejects, had had to make peace with the lifelong slog of life in India. Jignesh dropped out of college in the thirteenth year and joined his father's warehouse business. It was a dangerous line in a city perpetually strapped for space. Large warehouses attracted big attention, usually from the wrong crowd: cops, politicians and the underworld. Jignesh-bhai, as he was now popularly known, had earned his stripes at the age of twenty-two when he'd hired goons to beat up one of his father's troublesome clients. He had spent six months in prison for the crime. A small price to pay for a lifetime of priceless notoriety.

We were in his air-conditioned cabin. I had managed to catch him just in time. He was about to leave for home in his bullet-proof, chauffeur-driven Skoda. He tried to send me away, telling me to return the next morning. When I insisted the matter couldn't wait, he led me back into his cabin grudgingly.

'I need a gun,' I told him.

He laughed. 'Whom do you want to kill? The household rat?'

'No,' I said, taking a sip of the Thums Up he had ordered for me. 'I don't want to kill anyone or anything. I just want to scare someone.'

A smirk hung off Jignesh's fat face. He pushed his overweight body back in the executive leather chair. 'I don't have any gun-vun, Siraj, I'm not that sort...'

'Please, Jignesh. My father...' I said. 'He's being troubled by the neighbouring shop people. They park their car right outside our shop. Customers can't come in and my father... my father's just helpless!'

I hoped I'd hit a nerve with the father story.

'So you're going to threaten to kill them because they park badly?'

'They are Chilyas,' I explained to Jignesh. 'The only language they understand is a yank at their balls and a gun to their heads. If we don't show them first, they'll only become more daring!'

Jignesh finally parted with an unlicensed pistol which he brought out from behind the television mounted on his cabin wall. The weapon was dusty and looked like it hadn't been used in centuries. 'Bring it back as soon as you've finished your work,' he said.

I turned the piddly little thing around in my hands. 'How does it work?' I asked.

He pinned me with a cold stare. 'It doesn't.'

I should have insisted on one that did.

I hailed a taxi to Wadala. It was a trip I could barely afford. But given the circumstances, I was in no mood to travel by bus. The sky was darkening and the evening rush hour was getting worse by the second.

At the Dockyard Road circle, the cabbie tried to take the longer Byculla route.

I abused his mother and sister and told him to stick to the Sewri route.

It didn't go down well with the chap.

He abused my mother and sister right back and pulled over sharply. There was an outbreak of vehicle horns all around us. The cabbie didn't seem to care.

He turned his head and snarled, 'Get out, go catch another taxi.'

This was P. D'Mello road at 6.15 in the evening. He may as well have asked me to board a spaceship. The taxi's dashboard was crammed with idols of Hindu gods. We had stopped on the side of a crazily busy thoroughfare. Vehicles had to change lanes because of us.

'Don't make a fuss.' I said. 'Just keep going, and stick to the Sewri route as I told you.'

The cab driver was an older man, with greying hair and a black moustache. A red tilak shot upwards from between his unruly eyebrows. I didn't know then that this was an unforgiving snake of a man.

He let out a stream of abuses and ordered me to get out. I shouted back at him, telling him I wasn't going anywhere except to Wadala.

'Enough!' he said and banged on his steering wheel. He got out of the cab and slammed the door—hard enough to attract the attention of pedestrians. He came towards me through the right-side rear window. 'I said get out, your mother's cu...'

Jignesh's gun shut him up. I pointed it directly in the driver's face. 'Keep shut and get in. Get me to Wadala, and there won't be any more problems.'

He took in the gun and the sight of me holding it up. I half expected him to burst out laughing. Instead, he leapt back into his seat.

We reached Wadala Imax in what I thought was record-breaking time. It was almost seven.

While I paid him, the taxi driver asked if I would be long at the mall.

'What's it to you?' I said. The gun was making me intolerant of chit-chat.

'I was just asking, saab, in case you needed a ride back,' the driver said. 'I could wait around if that's the case.'

I glanced at the row of taxis idling outside the cineplex mall. This guy was clearly out of his head. 'Are you new to Mumbai?' I said. 'This is not your shitty Bihari village. Here no one waits for anyone. Get going.'

My mind was focused on the next roadblock in my way: the security check at the mall's entrance. It was manned by a puny woman and an undernourished-looking chap, both wearing identical uniforms: grey shirt, blue trousers and black tie.

I decided to brazen it out.

I passed through the metal detector without a beep. The female officer did a double take on seeing a gun on the tray. 'What is this, sir?' She pointed at the weapon as I reached out to retrieve it. The place was overrun by armies of mall rats.

I marvelled at the woman's discretion. There was a gun on her security-check tray and she was still trying to make sure.

'It's a lighter,' I said. I let the thing lie there on the tray between us. More people were lining up to go through the security check.

'No, sir, it is a gun,' she said.

'Lighter, madam. Lighter.'

'Light it and show,' she said.

'Gas is over,' I said.

'Arrey, come on, madam!' the man in line behind me interjected. 'Who would carry a gun so openly into a mall? It's a lighter. I know it. I also had one like this.'

I turned to look at my saviour. The usual corporate-type, portly and overdressed, with a plump wife and two impatient-looking teenaged kids in tow. The type who are usually killed first in terror attacks at five-star hotels. Or malls. 'How do you refill the gas in these things?' I asked the man.

He looked me over from head to toe. My leather slippers told him everything he needed to know. 'Arrey boss, you don't refill these things, you just throw them away and buy a new lighter.

They're just for… How much was it?' He turned to his wife, who shook her head to indicate she didn't remember the price of such inconsequential things. 'Anyway, just throw these lighters away. Don't carry around stuff like this and waste other people's time.'

He reached over from behind me. Before I could react, he had picked the gun off the tray. A quizzical look passed over his face. He eyed me fearfully as he weighed the gun in his hand.

'Gas is over,' I said, snatching it from his hands.

'Right,' he said, 'gas is over…'

The female security officer was reduced to impotent protests. 'Arrey but, sir… how can we allow… it looks so real… arrey, but…'

I pocketed the gun and sauntered off into the mall.

'Arrey but, sir, we cannot…' the security woman wailed to my back.

I was visiting a mall after a long time. I hadn't come to one since Gulshan was born. I don't know how Dilshad had formed the idea that parenthood had to be a morose, solemn eventuality. The Wadala mall, like all malls, had a festive look to it. As if everyday was the eve of some very special event or holiday. The Crossword bookshop, where Jaswant Plumber and her 'baby' were going to get the shock of their lives, was to the left.

I took the elevator to the third floor, to where the cineplexes were. I parked myself in the centre of a viewing gallery that overlooked the mall's entrance and main lobby. It was a beautiful vantage point from where I could see all those who came and went. Now all I had to do was wait for the two of you to show up.

I brought out your phone. The battery was running low. I was standing against the glass railing, with your phone in my hand and a sheer drop of fifty feet below. There were several missed calls and messages on your phone. What an in-demand dude you are, eh Rishad. With time to kill, I accessed your phone's image gallery.

Photos: of you at a restaurant with a group of friends; of some beautiful home that was too big to be in the city; of a young woman holding her tiny, just-born baby. Was this Deepika? Was this your child? I didn't care. I didn't want to see you as anything but the bastard who my wife addressed as 'baby'.

Photos: of you standing on the edge of a cliff, arms outstretched victoriously, with a bank of grey-black clouds on the distant horizon. Even though the images were small and grainy, I could imagine the cool wind at the edge of that cliff, the view at your feet, and the sense of abandon and leisure that you must have experienced being there. I envied you. I wanted your life. The cliff photos were dated two months ago. I tried to recall where I was around that time. Ah, yes: I'd spent that whole week in Nair Government Hospital, in the overcrowded General Ward, recovering from a bout of food poisoning.

I looked up. A gaggle of young girls streamed into the mall. They were all dressed in shorts and tank tops that revealed milky white legs and smooth arms. Hot women irritated me, as did everything else that I could never imagine possessing. Little did I know that even the little blob of pleasantness that I had dared to desire—and then marry—would be taken away from me. Rishad saab, I swore at that moment, if you are responsible for Dilshad leaving me, I will teach you the lesson of your life.

Your phone began beeping to indicate the battery was critically low. I stopped using it and just stood there against the glass railing, watching the traffic of people streaming in and out of the mall. I had no idea what I was going to do once you two arrived. Would I confront you both at Crossword? Would I force a confession out of you two at gunpoint? Or would I just throw away your cell phone in a trash bin and return to my life? My mind was undecided. Sometimes a man has to let moments determine their own destiny.

You walked in. Had it not been for the black helmet you carried like a pot of water, I might have missed you. You seemed taller and heftier than I remembered from the medical store earlier that day. Hand-to-hand combat was out of the question with you. You stood in the main foyer and looked around. You stopped a young couple and asked them something; they pointed in the direction of the bookshop.

At that precise moment, as if guided by divine hands, Dilshad drifted into the main foyer from the left. She must have used a side entrance. She walked directly into your path and you two encountered each other. I was seeing her after months. My heart started making strange movements. She was dressed in a kurta and jeans. She carried a huge handbag and was clutching her cell phone in her right hand. On seeing each other, your faces lit up. I watched you two as if I was dead already and spying on you from heaven.

Dilshad raised her arms, you leaned forward, and the two of you hugged. I witnessed all this impassively. She was pointing at her cell phone. You looked confused. She fingered her cell phone and held it up to your face. You read its contents and began shaking your head in disbelief. You brought out a cell phone from your shirt pocket and showed it to Dilshad. She shook her head and began making expressions of incredulity that just didn't suit her. You two looked around the main foyer. I stepped back from the glass railing. Both of you began fingering your respective phones.

I brought out your phone. It was flashing to indicate a text message. It was Jaswant Plumber. *Am here, Rishad, wher r u.*

And the next text was yours, from Deepika's number: *Am @ Crossword, boss, wher r u.*

I texted Jaswant Plumber: *Am in magazne section, on red sofa.*

Dilshad jumped on receiving my text. She showed it to you excitedly. The two of you set off towards the bookshop as if you both had a battle to fight.

I wish I could have executed my plan fully. It would have been a real Bollywood-style tamasha. *Jilted husband forces confession from estranged wife and lover at gunpoint.* And I would have demanded answers: Why Jaswant Plumber? Why Dilshad? Why me? But it was not to be. I was stupid to think I'd got away with carrying a gun into the mall so openly. Someone had been watching me all along.

Just as I was about to walk towards the elevators, a burly man in black shirt and jeans got out of one of them. 'Excuse me, sir!' he called out to me. He was followed by another identically dressed man. Fucking mall security.

I dashed off in the opposite direction, towards the stairway on the right.

'Hey, wait, you! Stop!' one of them yelled at my back.

I began running down the stairs with dangerous, reckless leaps.

The two men began chasing me down the stairway. I heard one of them say something. A walkie-talkie crackled back.

I darted across the main foyer. I bumped into people and pushed an elderly man to the floor.

'Catch him! He has a gun!' One of my pursuers yelled. The stupid fool.

There was pandemonium in the main foyer. People began running helter-skelter and in the ensuing chaos I managed to slip out of the structure.

I walked away from the air-conditioned mall into the humid night air.

I couldn't believe it. I couldn't believe how easily I'd escaped. I checked your phone. It had died.

With no more money to burn on taxi fare, I began walking towards the bus stop on the main road. It was a lonely deserted stretch once I left the gate of Bhakti Park. There was no pavement. I stuck to the sides of the road, skirting the undergrowth on the left. Beyond that lay the Mahul creek. It stank of rotting fish and shit.

The bus stop was a single pole with a flag-like sign indicating the bus number that serviced that route. A couple of cars passed. A few trucks.

I didn't notice the taxi until it came close. Its headlights were off. It slowed down as it approached. Three men jumped out as the taxi rolled past me. I didn't even have time to bring out Jignesh's useless gun. The three men pounced on me and pummelled me from all sides. They dragged me into the taxi's back seat.

It was the same taxi, the same statues of gods on the dashboard, the same green upholstery, and the same driver leering at me. 'Welcome back, chutiya! Had fun in the mall?'

The two men on either side of me continued to slap me and bash the back of my head. The taxi went down the road for about half a kilometre and then it took an abrupt left turn into the heart of the dark and ominous marshland.

We stopped at the edge of dry land. I could smell the sea all around. The sky was an orangish black.

They dragged me out of the taxi and slapped me and kicked me around for a long time. 'Will you point a gun at a taxi driver again?' they asked. 'Will you taunt his Bihari origin again?'

No, I cried, as I balled up on the ground. No. No. No. No. No. But it didn't lessen their punches.

One of them emptied my pockets. They tossed aside the phones and my wallet. It was Jignesh's gun they were after. They kept me face down on the muddy ground and stripped away my pants and underwear. They were laughing. They greased the gun, they greased me, and then while two of them held my legs apart, one of them… I screamed and screamed. You can't even begin to imagine pain of that magnitude. I passed out.

When I came to, the sky was bright. My body was in shock. Every time I moved, it felt like I was trying to crap a brick. I was lying in a drying pool of my own blood. I tried to fish out the gun, but the bastards knew what they were doing. They'd jammed the thing so deep in, I would have needed seven tong-shaped hands to perform the operation.

When I stood up, my eyes clouded over. I somehow got my trousers on. I gathered the phones and my wallet and then hopped and hobbled my way all the way to the main road.

I am writing this from Nair Hospital, where I am recovering from a very complicated surgery that required the expertise of three of the city's top proctologists. The police have the gun. They are also on the lookout for the cab driver and his friends who did this to me. I still have your cell phone. My mother managed to force a confession out of me about its true origin. She says God has punished me for my thievery. It is on her behest that I am writing to you. Please forgive me for stealing your phone. And please, before it causes me any more trouble, come and pick it up from General Ward IV on the second floor. I am in bed 28.

Siddhartha

WE are waking up.

To the clatter of rusty alarm clocks and the beep-beeps of short-lived China-made digital timepieces, we are being roused from our shallow sleep. It's impossible to be too restful before a journey. Many of us have been edgy all night, or for days or weeks; some have been starved of unconsciousness for most of our lives.

Our awakening has upset the ones we live with.

As we dart about our flats this morning, preparing to leave, the departure times for our various modes of transport marking each moment with panic, how our obstinacy must sting our cohabiters!

They ignore our requests for assistance in finding our socks or ironing our saree blouses. Their resentful glances make us spill our caffeinated beverages. We bathe and dress to the background score of sick-sick-sick, or, I-can't-believe-this.

As we are about to walk out of our doors, with our backpacks or handbags or medium-sized suitcases, the ones we live with tell us to go to hell. They ask what we mean by taking off like this, on what grounds, with what understanding. Seriously, who do we think we are!

(Over the past months and years, we've gone missing from the daily grind for hours on end, often for whole afternoons or weekends. But this time, with this trip, we will be gone too far and for too long.)

We glance down, at the watches of various sizes and brands adorning our respective wrists. There isn't time enough. And so we exhale and put forward our reasons for the ten zillion thousandth time.

We tell the ones we live with that we have a right to, or that we feel a burning need to, or that we have no idea why we want to...

We are not allowed to finish. Our incomplete sentences are yanked from us, and by now, after countless such exchanges, we have ceased to be enraged by the unintended meanings wrought upon our unspoken words.

We have a right to... *be escapists?*

We feel a burning need to... *jump town like circus clowns, with no sense of responsibility for jobs (or studies or spouses or parents or children...)?*

We check the time again, this time surreptitiously, on the clocks on the walls past the shoulders of those we live with. If we don't leave in two minutes, we'll never make it. Or maybe we'll reach in time to watch our trains or buses or long-distance taxis pulling away like satellites with other gravitational obligations.

Why aren't you listening! We are startled by the volume and get ready to be struck. Instead, more verbal punches ensue: *Why are you being so heartless!*

Within their soundproof cages of flesh and bone, our affronted cardiac muscles thump in protest.

We say we don't like being screamed at. We say our minds are made up—which is not entirely true, since the distress of those trying to hold us back makes us yearn for the days when it had never occurred to us to go.

Now we are pressing the elevator buttons. Those of us who live close to the ground are running down the stairs or are already on the streets outside our apartment buildings. Some of our names are being yelled from windows and doors or building lobbies. We are being called bastards and bitches and sissies and pathetic fools even as we are ducking into cabs or autorickshaws.

We tell ourselves that goodbyes like these are a privilege. We imagine we are lucky to be loved so fiercely.

The expressions of those driving us to our points of departure indicate otherwise.

It is a crushingly hot October morning.

Among the garrulous multitudes jostling about us at railway stations, at bus depots or at outstation taxi stands, we hope there are at least a few others headed where we are. Our need to be accompanied is incurable. We expect arms to be stretched out for us endlessly as we dangle over life's ravines and forests.

Arms which we must later hack off when they won't pull back or let go, like earlier this morning.

We take our seats. Our journeys are about to commence. Around some of our necks are chains with alphabetical pendants or lockets that enclose photographs of sweethearts or deities. Our bags contain music players, laptops, diaries, magazines, packaged food items, toiletries of staggering inconsequentiality… Except for our clothes, we will require almost none of these things where we are going.

Fellow passengers look engrossed in thoughts about the people and plans awaiting them at the end of their trip. We scrutinize them in an attempt to glean their destinations. Are any of them free-falling like us? Is anyone going where we are?

Our co-passengers notice us observing them. We trade nods and smiles; and then we ask one another, in numerous languages and in a variety of ways, a similar sort of question:

Aap kahaan jaa rahey ho?

Tamey kyan jao chho?

Where are you headed?

Off to my parents', someone says. For a vacation, someone else says. I've just been released from prison, another person says, after six long years, regretting my crime every second I spent behind bars. And you?

And you? they ask again.

We don't answer. In light of the ceaseless coming and going of countless people across the length and breadth of this vast subcontinent, our journeys must appear to be yet another meaningless excursion.

Our mass-transit vehicles pick up speed.

For the remainder of our journeys, we strive to extract pleasure from all the mundane rituals of travel. From this evening onwards, for days to come, even the simplest joys will be out of our reach—a touch, a song, a taste of our favourite treat…

And so we daydream, eat, read, watch videos, play music, and gaze out of the windows of our mass-transit vehicles with the absorption of toddlers.

Where we are going, there will be such austerity, such deprivation. We have our reasons for going; at least it's our decision, it's what we chose. Decades from now, what may (or may not) be a fiery post-petroleum planet, such austerity, we have been assured, may no longer be optional.

Hong Kong sex workers drug and rob tourists.

Mumbai mayor's plea to drive out hawkers falls on deaf ears.

US plans Gitmo closure, new rights for detainees.
Indian in race for Citi's top slot.
Will high crude prices spoil Dalal Street party?
Kashmiri youth rediscover religion.
GodTube.com a hit with the religious.
Nalbandian is the Master of Paris.
Drowsy drivers a road hazard in the US.
More than 3,500 Chinese babies named 'Olympics'.
Blanchett confirms pregnancy.
Christina is pregnant.
Foreigner nabbed with smack.
Diwali crackers kill one.
Comet dazzles stargazers...

Vacating our seats at the end of our journey, we leave our newspapers behind. When yet another torrent of trivia piles up outside homes throughout the nation tomorrow morning, we will, mercifully, be spared the daily societal guilt—of being over-informed, yet remaining so utterly unmoved.

Upon our arrival at our destination at various times through the day, each of us is given an envelope in which to deposit our mass-produced and commonly owned possessions.

Many of us require two envelopes, and some ask for three. They are sealed before our eyes and locked away in cupboards.

This place we've come to is on a hill. It is full of tree-lined gravel walkways that wind past the dining areas, our residential quarters and two vast halls in which we will spend up to fourteen hours a day braving nullity.

Had we been less distressed by our separation from our things, we would've noticed how spectacular this place is; we would've been grateful for the chilly mountain air and the gorgeous landscape views that play peekaboo with the thick foliage.

But without our cell phones, MP3 players, laptops, cameras, cigarettes, paan masala packets, jewellery, cash... denied of these essentials, which the people who run this place have deemed too valuable or dangerous or unnecessary for us to possess in here, we feel weakened, like walls with missing bricks.

It comes as some relief to finally be among others like us; actually, scores of others like us, who've left behind their homes, responsibilities, debts and deadlines to experience the utter denial of the world that is engineered in this place.

The families, couples and groups of friends who've come here together are holding their last conversations.

Wasn't that an STD booth we spotted outside the gate on our way in?

Now, with barely an hour left before our tongues are stilled by vows of silence, we rush out to make our final phone calls.

The line at the phone booth is long.

The woman presiding over it is wise, ensuring every call ends in under two minutes.

We all get to speak. We get to hear the voices of those whose shouts and invectives saw us off this morning. There is no more rage or bitterness. There is just mutual concern. Some of us hear weeping at the other end of the lines. It makes us want to die. *Oh come on*, we say with mock nonchalance, *it's no big deal, it's just ten days*!

Ten days, 240 hours, 0.04 per cent of seventy-year lifespans. We have seen lives change in two seconds and we will be gone for 864,000 of them.

Time's up.

...make sure you shut the gas properly; tell him I'll send the cheque

as soon as I'm back; take your medication regularly; cross the road carefully; don't let her get to you; don't take that route; don't sleep with anyone new; I love you; I'll miss you; I'll see you soo…

TIME'S UP!

Our stroll back—from the phone booth to the entrance of the centre—turns out to be the most mournful sixty feet any of us has ever traversed.

What we spoke into the phone—maudlin terms of affection and anxiety—will be the last utterances to escape our lips for days to come.

We return to our rooms. We close the doors. We push our bags under our beds and sit down on the meagre mattresses and wait, like prisoners, for the gong that will announce the start of our severance from life, as we know it.

For the second time today, our hearts are beating so fast they could flee this place if they had legs.

We're amassed outside the two halls assigned to our respective sexes, waiting to be called in. In the distance one can hear the rumble of highway traffic and the bugles of passing trains. The sun has just set.

How did we not notice! There are not just scores, but hundreds of others like us here. They—or rather we—are old and young and rich and poor and rural and urban. So many of us are from foreign lands. For the next ten days, while eating, walking, sitting and living together in absolute silence, we will play guessing games with ourselves about our fellow attendees' lives, their origins.

With hundreds of tongues on hold, the only sounds are of crows and bulbuls and the sharp chirps of unseen creatures.

Yesterday, right about now, many of us were at home, dining

with our families in front of television sets. Some of us were out shopping for knick-knacks—torches, mosquito repellents, warm clothing. Several of us were still at work, struggling to complete assignments before we took leave. Until yesterday, despite our preparations, our going away was as yet tinged with uncertainty. Even on the eve of our departure, we didn't think we were the kind who could turn away from the world, even if for just ten days, even though our needlessness in this world had been revealed to us over time in sharp excruciating instalments. 'Mother', 'father', 'banker', 'doctor', 'teacher', 'brother', 'student', 'boss'... all these ephemeral labels and their demands on our lives that we have put on hold to be here.

Through the mosquito-netted windows of the halls, we catch a glimpse of the endless rows of blue 3×3 mattresses arranged like cavalry inside. In there is a spot assigned to each one of us.

People claim their lives are infused with meaning after spending ten days here. They say the scars of their past are erased by this drill. Upon returning to their daily routine, they find themselves centred and unshakeable, no less.

We've come here, despite such alarming testimonies, because we have been lured by something more prosaic than the promise of some dubious peace.

We are beneficiaries of a rare variety of charity at this centre. Each of us is being fed and housed by the direct contributions of those who were here before us. When we leave, we will be expected to do likewise for those who come after us. How much we part with in the end will depend on how deeply we desire to perpetuate this centre and its teachings. Our scepticism is non-negotiable; we might end up shelling out nothing. But by providing free shelter and sustenance, even to those who could afford to pay five times over, this centre has bestowed on us something extraordinary—an opportunity to spend a few days on this planet untainted by the twin stains of profit and loss. For many of us, this was reason enough.

Girish Khanna! *Kasim Pilani*! *Nick Fischer*! *Rahul Adhikari*!

And, on the ladies' side:

Rajni Chani! *Mila Rutso*! *Avantika Joshi*! *Minaz Khwaja*!

We break away from the crowds upon hearing our names and venture into the halls one by one.

By the time the last woman and man have been called in, it is night.

The lights outside the halls are switched off.

Where hundreds of us were standing half an hour ago, there is now empty darkness.

I feel a motion gurgling through my lower intestines. A couple of seconds later, the liquid mess comes gushing out into the adult diaper wrapped around my lower end. The goo squelches to the front to my genitals. They call this *addhittana* up there in the meditation centre on the hill, this state of determined immobility regardless of what the body goes through. The *addhittana* ends after an hour. My *addhittana*, on the other hand…

'I could smell it all the way down,' my brother says, as he enters the room. I have been lying on my side, facing the window. My brother turns me away from the window and onto my back. I can no longer see the meditation centre. Now my vista is the patchy ceiling of my brother's top-floor bedroom in his dilapidated, illegally occupied row house. My brother lifts my legs and dabs my behind with a piece of damp newspaper. He uses several more pieces of the same dampened newspaper to wipe the excreta off my private parts. I thought it would get easier with time. Shock over my body's treachery had given way to acceptance. Now I am just furious at my imprisonment in this paralysed and sore-ridden rack of flesh and bones.

I hear the gong go off at the centre. Bedtime for them. I had worked at that centre for a few months in my youth. It was a rite of passage for the village youngsters, to work there for free food and peanuts as pay before deciding that one needed to escape from this quiet humble village life. Most returned as very rich men or as crematoria remains. No one had returned like I had, as a penniless and immobile slab of living flesh.

'I'll bring your dinner in half an hour,' my brother says. Before going away, he turns me on my side again so I can look out of the window. The meditation centre is dark. The requisite to working there was a compulsory eleven-day course. I was nineteen then. I knew I was being watched closely by the centre management. I behaved like the ideal sadhak: obedient, restrained and punctual. Whenever I missed home, I would come to the edge of the hill and look down at my village and try to locate my family's cottage among the jumble of similar cottages. I remember my first successful *addhittana*, the sense of achievement at having sat immobile for an hour, while my skin crawled with unscratched itches and my lower back felt like it was on fire. I remember that afternoon on the seventh day, halfway into the *addhittana*, the air around me suddenly felt liquid, I half opened my eyes and saw things seeming hazy, there but not there, and I, the witness, felt removed from ordinary time, felt like I had been reinstated into something eternal and ever-present. I should have kept working at that centre. I have wasted decades of my life seeking fulfilment and riches in cities around the country, only to end up where I started. Annicca, the main teacher at that centre, used to say hundred times a day. Impermanence. Annicca. Impermanence.

My brother's wife comes up. Dinner time. If I could speak

I would order them to stop feeding me, let this body die away. She turns me away from the window and props my head up with a pillow. She opens my jaw and sticks a spoonful of daal into my mouth. My tongue remains unresponsive. The daal trickles down to my throat. My heart starts racing. I could drown in the liquid. But something inside the body still hasn't forgotten protocol. The daal trickles down the right passage. My ravenous stomach leaps up to my gullet and drags the liquid down to its cavernous innards. My sister-in-law shovels spoon upon spoon into my mouth.

My mind soars to the centre on the hilltop. Tonight I am a sadhak again, lying in *addhittana* until I die.

We, the Happy

THERE are no more youngsters left. We send our children away to America, Australia, the UK, Canada… They go there, alone or with their spouses. They obtain degrees and slog like dogs and send us a few hundred dollars or pounds each month to run our households. We spend most of that foreign currency on medicines. We are so old, so riddled with ailments. But we are happy. We are relieved that our children have managed to escape the quagmire of this corrupt and unjust nation. They keep calling us abroad; they tell us to move there with them. We go visit. But we can never think of staying back there. We consider it our duty to remain in India and tend to the properties that our children will inherit after our death. Maybe we can enjoy the clean air and comfort of foreign nations in some other life. In this life, this is where we must live and this is where we must die.

We will be troublesome in our death. Upon receiving the news of our demise, our children will have to drop everything and pay through their nose for last-minute air tickets. While our bodies decay in morgues, our children must undertake the painful flight back home, where there will be nothing but grief and tedium awaiting them: the necessity of transporting our bodies from the hospital to the graveyard/cremation ground, the formality of facing herds of relatives, the rituals of our funerals. And then there will be the headache of dealing with lawyers and having titles transferred and becoming responsible for the upkeep of properties that are finally theirs. In anticipation of our death, we already regret not having moved abroad when our children had asked us to. Maybe in another life we will be less anxious about things like home and roots.

We are aware that we are the last generation in many ways. We are the last generation to live and die exclusively in India. The last generation to have parents who didn't speak English. The last generation to believe that happiness is not a personal individual state, but rather the fulfilment of duties and obligations that create a state of happiness, not necessarily one's own. Our children don't understand this. They think we are masochists, fools with a martyr complex, obsessed with fulfilling formalities and bending backwards to conform to social norms. It's true that we lack the ability to say no, enough, this much and no more. But it is this reed-like plasticity that allows us to cling to our properties, to spend conservatively and to endure the absence of our children with brave, smiling faces. If we became the sort of people our children want us to be, they would be the first casualties of our fierce individualism.

Nothing gives us more joy than to learn that our children have acquired property abroad. When they tell us the price of these homes, our minds stagger at the equivalent amount in rupees. More than the affluence of our children, what awes us is the idea that a piece of land in another part of the world is under our indirect ownership. Yes, our children are ours, just as we are theirs, and whatever is theirs is ours by extension. The awareness of their overseas properties inflates our sense of the self, it makes us feel less angry about the petty, inconsequential lives that we have endured in this petty, insufferable nation.

We hate India. Any nation in the world is better than ours.

We don't mean to be outrageous. At our age, there is too much experience propping up each thought, each statement. We know India well enough to despise it. We dread the idea of being born here again, of having to undergo another cycle of existence in this deplorable nation. When our children were growing up, we didn't care what they became—doctors, lawyers, engineers, artists—it didn't matter, as long as they went away. At times our children misunderstood our insistence. They thought we were trying to get rid of them. That might be true. But at least we were exiling them to lands of fresh water, clean air, wholesome food and fair societies.

Nothing hurts us more than to hear our children complain about their lives abroad. They whine about the extreme weather, the hard work, the loneliness, the lack of leisure. They threaten to return home, to India. In moments of anger, during phone calls or during visits, they dare us to go experience the emptiness of their overseas lives. Emptiness. We hear that word a lot from them. The longer our children live away, the more this cancerous concept comes preying on their minds, their moods, their hearts. Our scepticism or inability to understand only makes them furious. Life isn't just about big homes and big cars, they try to explain to us, as if we are to blame for their bottomless desire for more money, more things or more admiration from their peers. We know it is our duty to listen, to stoically bear the misdirected outbursts of our children until they've vented their rage and are once again composed enough to take on the demands of their Western lives. To be a parent these days is to be a psychic garbage dump. When our children threaten to return to India, it terrifies us like nothing else. We will endure any amount of unjust nastiness to ensure that our children never come back here. We've lived alone for too long to tolerate their presence for longer than the duration of a vacation.

Without our children, our days have a mellow predictability to them. We seldom leave home. We never go shopping. Everything we need is brought to our doorsteps by a number of service providers who have become surrogate children over the years. The milkman, the maid, the vegetable vendor, the bread seller, all these people who take our money and give us so much more in return than just their goods and services. On the rare occasions that we are absent from our daily routines, these are the people we miss the most: their arrival, their familiar clothes and peculiar smells and specific ways of speaking that have become endearing to us over time. If we are not careful, one day someone from this large universe of doorstep service providers will force their way into our homes, tie us up to furniture, and proceed to burgle our belongings. Should we make too much of a racket, a hammer or a metal rod will be used to knock us unconscious, or even kill us. When our bodies are discovered, some hours or days later, we will make headlines for a few days, and then we will become one more digit in the city's senior citizen attack statistic. We know several of our cohorts who've gone this way. We try to forget them as quickly as we can.

Life is beautiful. Despite corrupt governments, starving children, water and food shortages, police extortion, outrageous inflation, and even despite brutal senior citizen murders, yes, life is beautiful. This is how we wish to perceive the world as we prepare to leave it, although our children will be sure to disagree with our rosy exit reviews. We wish we could be around, at least in spirit if not in body, to know what our children think of the world towards the end of their own stay in it.

As the underlying fragility of our bodies becomes more evident with each passing day, we find it astonishing that we've managed to survive for so long, dodging the diseases, accidents, calamities and wars that have taken the lives of countless others. Why them and not us? It's not like our extended stay on this planet has made things better. If anything, we've only been taking up space. So many of us died so long ago, when we stopped working, or reading, or when we lost a partner, or left a partner, or when we ceased to trust and turned into cobras with splayed hoods, stubbornly coiled atop the keys to our middle-class kingdoms, guarding our properties, bank accounts and safes against our relatives, friends, and worse, our own children.

It isn't easy for us to let go. Behind each and every rupee we've made and saved is a harrowing tale of succeeding against the odds. It is only par for the course that we keep things difficult for others. And so, we never make payments or bestow gifts without first belittling the recipient. The pettier the amount, the harsher our words. The sweeper boys and garbage collectors have it worst.

Coming to age in a brand new nation, in the decades after independence, we felt a moral responsibility to be successful. Prolonging the pre-colonial poverty seemed like an affront to the shining post-colonial future that had been bestowed upon us. The old rich grew richer. And the economically restless? We turned into money-hungry fiends who would do anything we could to fatten our own wallets. The world is littered with victims of our underhanded dealings and unkept financial promises—our horrified friends, heartbroken siblings, shocked colleagues and dismayed relatives. That's probably why we rarely step out of our multimillion-rupee flats. Infirmity is our excuse to stay away from the familiar street corners and buildings where memories of our transgressions come alive with painful clarity.

Thankfully, the old world is being razed, and with it the mise en scènes of our misdeeds. We can see from our windows that a new city, a new India, is being birthed. Impossibly tall skyscrapers have begun blotting out the horizon. Newspapers carry tales of the new pleasures on offer: air-conditioned shopping malls, multi-screen cinema halls, fast-food chain stores, and street-side cultural festivals open to one and all. We are all for the new. Redevelop! Rebuild! Let old streets be renamed and let centuries-old landmarks be obliterated to make way for flyovers and traffic roundabouts. As survivors of the past decades, we can testify that there is nothing worth preserving. Kitsch-revering youngsters may bemoan all they want the passing of Irani cafés and double-decker buses; let them print images of koli women and bullock carts on their expensive T-shirts. The quicker things change, the more sorely they are missed. But change is inevitable. It is moral! Our dying wish? That the world we depart from be nothing like the world we arrived in.

We will not succumb to the temptation to describe the world we arrived in. Having been youngsters once, we know the dreariness of the elderly trudging down memory lane. Our pasts don't occupy our minds nearly as much as thoughts of our inevitable death—not the when of it, but the how. We are hoping against hope that the dissonance in our lives will have no bearing on the pitch of our last moments. We don't want to die gasping for air, with tubes and needles stuffed up our orifices and arms. We don't want the last sounds we hear to be the frenetic beeps of ECG machines announcing to the world the cessation of our individual, irreparable hearts. But it doesn't matter what we don't want. We shall reap as we sowed and go as we lived: breathlessly, violently, ravaged by struggle and torn apart by our desire for more money, more respect, more security, and in the end, more life, more life, more life...

By the time our children turn up to claim our bodies, bedraggled from their transcontinental journeys, our glaciated faces will reveal nothing about the horror of our last moments. *Papa went peacefully,* our children will deduce from the serenity of our countenance, *Mummy went in peace.* As if that were a mark of a life well lived—even if it were true.

Balance Sheet

THE son rode with his father's body from the hospital to the graveyard. He never thought he had it in him to be locked up in the back of an ambulance with a corpse. He almost sat with the ambulance driver and his assistant in the front. But a sudden desire to be seen as responsible made him queasy about leaving his father's corpse alone. He imagined his father being shaken about as the vehicle navigated the city's pothole-ridden roads. The dead man's son didn't want to be blamed for any mishap.

He waited for the ambulance team and a hospital wardboy to strap his father in place. After they got off, he clambered into the back of the ambulance. They slammed the door shut and locked it from outside. The son had asked for an air-conditioned ambulance for his father's last ride through this city. It was a final treat for a man who had shunned all comforts in the last years of his life. He would have vehemently disapproved of the two thousand rupees being spent on the transportation of a mere corpse—even if it were his own. The son wanted to undo the dead man's self-depriving stance; it was the only way he could enjoy himself in this world that his father had just left. So now he and his father were sealed in a cool, soundproof bubble as the ambulance began its slow trundle to the Shia Imami Ismaili Kabrastan five kilometres away.

It was probably the hottest afternoon of the year. An entire stretch of the road outside the hospital had been barricaded for repair. The traffic in the area was impossible, as it was in the rest of this overcrowded city by the coast. It was going to be a long day. The burial would be followed by evening prayers at the jamatkhana, and then a rudimentary bhaati dinner of daal, rice and pickle for relatives and acquaintances. It was the same ritualistic send-off for every Ismaili Khoja.

In the back of the ambulance, from opposite walls, jutted two planks. The dead man's son sat in the centre of one; the father lay stretched out on the other. It was already 1.30 p.m. The mayat was scheduled to begin in two hours. The son hoped there would be enough time for the dargah committee to prepare his father's body. He thought of phoning his wife, to tell her he had finally set off from the hospital. He thought of phoning his mother, to tell her the same thing. But he was tired of calling and arranging and informing and consoling. He silenced his phone and put it away. He decided he would luxuriate in the peaceful coolness of the ambulance till the ride ended.

His father's body was tightly wrapped in a white sheet, revealing the familiar contours of his arms, his hips, his feet. The knot had been tied on top of the head of all places, lending an air of silliness to the whole attempt to conceal the corpse. The body jiggled and trembled every time the ambulance drove over an obstacle. The leather straps across his father's chest and knees were pulled tight, preventing the body from shifting around too much. The son hoped the straps would hold.

He hadn't touched his father since he'd died the previous night. The family was called in once the ICU staff had finished cleaning up all proof of the violent and bloody resuscitation effort. The son had noticed signs of it all around his father's bed and on the clothing of the nurses and doctors on duty. By the time the family was allowed in, however, his father's corpse had been wrapped in a pristine white sheet. The face had been left uncovered for the benefit of relatives. An older relative had clucked his tongue when he saw that the dead man's eyes were open; he shot out a hand to smooth down this sign of a painful death. Or so the belief went: Those who struggled against death usually died with open eyes. The son knew his father must have suffered immensely. A cardiac arrest couldn't have been a pleasant way to go. And the resuscitation effort must have been worse: the tearing apart of a man's ribcage, the slapping around of his flailing heart, the attachment of the pacemaker, the steroid injections.

The son shifted his gaze from the ambulance window down to his father's corpse. He wished he had asked for the face to be uncovered for the duration of the ride. He thought of doing it himself, of loosening the silly knot on his father's head and parting the sheet just a little to unveil his visage. But he feared it might be deemed inappropriate by the relatives and dargah committee members who were waiting to receive the body at the kabrastan. The son had never really cared for or understood community rituals and, at a time like this, he was all too afraid of flouting some well-established norm. With his father's face covered, he found it difficult to invoke any tenderness towards the corpse. He rode with it like he was in a train compartment, sitting across from someone's sack of potatoes.

The ambulance driver was taking the shortest and most dramatic route to the kabrastan. It cut across the breadth of the city, from the elite Hindu-dominated western seaboard, where the hospital was, to the Muslim ghetto in the downmarket east, which was crammed tight with decaying buildings, mosques and graveyards. The city's residents didn't usually have reason to traverse this route. The easterners mostly remained mired in their parts of town, and the westerners swished about in theirs. His father's life had been an attempt to claw himself out of the east and get to the west. He had partially succeeded. He had managed a residence in the centre of town, and a professional practice that allowed him to rub shoulders with the city's best. And now, after having breathed his last on the thirtieth floor of a sea-facing hospital, surrounded by buildings with multimillion-rupee homes, his father was being transported back to where he'd started, to be laid to rest in the neighbourhood he had spent his life fleeing.

To hell with it. The son knelt down on the floor of the ambulance and began struggling with the knot on his father's head. It turned out to be deceptive, with the loose ends of the cloth disappearing mysteriously down the back of his father's neck. He stuck his hand under his father's right shoulder. He realized he was touching his father. The body was ice-cold. It had been stored all night in the hospital's morgue. He finally found the edge of the cloth. He began pulling it out. As the knot on the head unravelled and the cloth came away, he found he had uncovered his father's face right down to his bare shoulders.

The son remained kneeling, his face just a couple of feet from his father's. The nostrils had been plugged with cotton balls. Some sort of yellow chemical coated the hair and skin; this was probably what made the corpse odourless. Dad, he thought. Dad. There was no scope here for self-pity or sentimentality. The son knew that at that precise moment there were probably hundreds of sons transporting their fathers' corpses in ambulances across the country. That was the advantage of living in an overpopulated nation: the individual experience could be made pedestrian in an instant by setting it against the collective. Have you been raped?

So have millions. Robbed? So have millions. Are you happy? Furious? Successful? So are millions. People often underwent the most bizarre and remarkable experiences without realizing the extraordinariness of what they'd just been through. Like the son kneeling on the floor of the ambulance and gazing into his dead father's face, communing this closely with his father's corpse without breaking down or being overwhelmed by nostalgia. The dead always have lessons to teach. There he was, kneeling on the floor of the ambulance, imbibing every precious nugget of ineffable wisdom that seemed to emanate from his father's corpse. The son passed his hand over his father's head. The hair felt sticky and matted. He flinched.

He wiped his hand on his jeans and sat back on the plank. He reached over and re-draped the white sheet over his father's face. He felt like he'd woken up from a dream. This is why we get rid of our dead, he realized, because otherwise they begin to mesmerize the living. For the rest of the journey, he ignored the corpse, regarding it with a sideways glance.

The ambulance passed under the JJ Bridge, the unofficial border marking the start of the Muslim precincts. Here the municipal neglect was breathtaking. Both sides of the roads were lined with restaurants, chai shops and miscellaneous businesses. The pavements were overrun by hawkers and beggars, forcing pedestrians to walk alongside the vehicular traffic. The area looked like it was stuck in a mediaeval time warp. Burkha-clad women jostled with skull-capped old men as they made their way around heaps of garbage or a supine overweight goat with a rope tied around its neck. The dead man's son watched all this from the ambulance. Sixty years ago, the dead man must have been one of those dusty-faced barefoot boys in ill-fitting clothes who even today played on the little patch of pavement below their crumbling apartment building. The ambulance drove past his father's favourite fast-food joint. It drove past the building he'd grown up in. It drove past the row of sweet shops from where his father would bring fondly remembered childhood treats—oily, overly rich confections that his cosmopolitan family dismissed as too heavy to imbibe. And finally, the ambulance heaved its way over the speed-breaker that had been installed to slow down hearses before they entered the gate of the kabrastan.

There were scores of landmarks that the ambulance had left out; they lay hidden in the area's by-lanes: the main jamatkhana where the dead man and his wife had married; the building where the couple had first lived before beginning their ascent up the city's real-estate ladder. The son remembered the ground-floor flat where his father's old aunt had lived until nine years ago. Upon receiving news of her death, his father had said that an entire era had ended with her. She was the oldest surviving relative his father had known. Now that his own father had died, the son thought he began to understand a little bit about eras coming to an end. But where his father had seemed moved at that old lady's demise, all the son felt now, riding with his father's corpse, was a certain nonchalance. Some eras were best finished.

The kabrastan was a seven-acre oasis of tranquility surrounded by tragic-looking apartment buildings. Many considered it lucky to live overlooking a graveyard. But none of that luck reflected in the condition of their ramshackle flats. The coconut trees in the kabrastan were the tallest in the city. The almond and mango trees were known to bear the most delicious fruits people ever tasted. Rich with the rot of almost two centuries of human flesh and blood, the soil of this kabrastan was probably the most fertile that ever existed.

The ambulance wound its way past the cobbled courtyard where a defunct water fountain gathered dust in the centre. Male relatives and acquaintances would circle this fountain five times, carrying his father's coffin on their shoulders. The son had attended funerals in the past where men had practically rioted for a chance to shoulder the janazah. He didn't foresee such a situation arising in his father's case. His father, quite frankly, was not the sort to invoke hysteria in others.

Five men—three uncles and two cousins—were seated on chairs in the courtyard under the shade of a corpulent neem tree. When they saw the ambulance, they stopped their conversation. The cousins began following the ambulance as it trundled past. The vehicle slowed to a crawl and came to a complete stop at the stairs of the viewing room. The ambulance driver seemed to know his way around the place. Inside the ambulance, the son was wishing the ride had lasted longer. He had never spent so much time in his father's presence in such silence. He heard the door of the driver's cabin open and close. In those few seconds it took the ambulance driver to come around to the back, the son recited a salwaat and patted his father's knees. Hang in there, he thought, the worst is behind you.

The cousins peered in as soon as the door opened. They studied the son's face closely as he climbed out of the ambulance. The son had been noticing this look on his relatives' faces since the previous night. He realized they were looking for some sign of emotion, on the ready to console him. But the situation hadn't risen as yet. The son had discovered an inability to express grief in public. On being formally informed of his father's death by the ICU head of staff, he had felt the enormous reality of life descend on him, like a gigantic and fragile soap bubble resting lightly on his head. It plunged him into a pensive, injured state of mind. It was only five hours later, after he'd deposited his father in the hospital's cold storage and returned home at 2 a.m. that the soap bubble had begun to thin. He had caved in the moment he lay down in bed and wrapped his arms around his wife's pregnant belly. He had howled and howled into the anonymous blankness of her swollen breasts.

'You all right?' Cousin 1 asked.

The dead man's son was disoriented on re-entering the breathtaking afternoon heat. The cold air escaped the ambulance like a freed genie.

Members of the dargah committee—five young Ismaili men—took over immediately. They began discussing how best to bring the body out and carry it in.

Cousin 2: 'Why aren't you picking up your phone?'

The son dug out his phone from his pocket. 'It's on silent,' he said. 'Why?' His eyes darted from face to face as Cousins 1 and 2 looked at each other.

'Why? What happened?' the son asked.

'Why don't you just check your phone?' Cousin 1 said.

The son saw twenty-two missed calls: they were from his wife, from a couple of uncles and aunts, from these cousins, from his mother, and from several unidentified numbers—probably belonging to neighbours or other relatives who had currently colonized the dead man's flat.

There were nine text messages too; again from an assortment of senders, each subsequent message growing more urgent, more alarming.

It became immediately clear to the son: He would have to miss his own father's funeral. Only an insane person would choose to grieve at a time like this.

He looked up at his cousins in bewilderment. 'This wasn't supposed to happen for at least fifteen days...'

'It must be the stress…' Cousin 1 said.

The son glanced in the direction of the viewing room, where his father's body was being carried in by the dargah committee. The ambulance driver and his assistant were drinking water from a tap. They seemed relieved that their day was almost done.

'What do I do now?' the son asked. He didn't want to seem too eager to abandon the duties at hand.

'What kind of question is that!' Cousin 2 shot back. 'Your father's already gone, he doesn't need you any more. You cannot be here at such a time!' Cousin 2's certainty in a situation like this was not surprising. Both of this cousin's kids—Ahad, five, and Shazia, two—had been born in his absence in New York. On both occasions, a couple of months before delivery, their Green-Card-holding mother had flown to be with her parents in America to give birth to American citizens. For the first three months of their lives, while they were still too young for the rigours of the New York–Mumbai flight, Cousin 2's kids were to him mere non-corporeal digital simulations whom he could see, on videoconferencing and in photographs, but never smell or hold.

'But this wasn't supposed to happen so soon!' The son realized he was repeating himself. 'The doctor had given us a date fifteen days from today.'

The three uncles gathered around. They were all in agreement: The dead man's son ought to leave right away. 'Your father would have done the same thing,' one of the uncles said. 'He was so practical. Always no-nonsense and doing whatever had to be done.'

The dead man's son looked around the kabrastan, at the courtyard, the mosque and, in the distance, the wild profusion of tall, dark-green trees that derived nourishment from the burial ground. He had attended numerous funerals at this kabrastan since he was a young boy, starting with his grandmother's when he was seven years old. Over the years he had shouldered the coffins of uncles, aunts, neighbours, of young men who had been killed in accidents, and of young women who had died of mysterious illnesses. He always wondered what it was like to be the immediate kin of the deceased. Now he would never know if the elaborate Ismaili funeral rituals provided genuine and lasting succour to the aggrieved, or whether these rituals were just a ploy to divert the mourners' minds from morbid, self-pitying thoughts. Like going to a film or hitting a bar.

He dialled his wife's number. An aunt answered. His wife was in no condition to talk. 'Come fast!' the aunt urged. 'Come to the hospital right now! They are about to take her to the delivery room…'

The son rushed to the viewing room. He wanted to see his father one last time. There was one more thing he would never know: the weight of his father's janazah. Behind a wooden partition, his father's corpse was being washed by three dargah committee men. They had turned his father on his stomach and were scrubbing his naked back. The son's phone began flashing again. This would have to be it where his father was concerned. He prayed one more salwaat and rushed out to take the phone call.

It was his wife. She sounded calm. She was crowning. She could feel her insides making way. She was sorry for doing this to him at a time like this.

He told her not to be ridiculous. He was on his way.

The ambulance was still parked outside the viewing room. The dead man's son waved to his cousins and uncles from a distance. They goaded him to rush. He began walking towards the kabrastan's gate as fast as he could. The further he walked from the viewing room, the more he pitied the father he was abandoning to the care of strangers. The uncle was wrong. His father would have never fled a parent's funeral. But the son was not his father. Tears trickled down his face and dripped into his grinning mouth. There was an excruciating tickle in the pit of his stomach. He wanted to get to the hospital as soon as he could. Nothing else mattered now. His dead father, the grief, the memories, the obligations. There was a lifetime ahead to make right on the choices of these moments. There was a new life knocking at the world's door five kilometres away.

The son burst into a jog to cover the last few yards.

He passed under the kabrastan's gate and sprinted across the broken-down pavement.

He swerved around a trio of blind beggars who were singing.

And then the dead man's son ran smack into what was possibly the gridlock of the century.

Nothing moved—the cars, the taxis, the tempos, the motorcyclists, and marooned amid them all like a beached whale was a single-decker BEST bus. The son looked around in panic. All the taxis were taken. All the private cars had their windows up. There was a cacophony of honking from the traffic intersection at the end of the road. But here, right outside the kabrastan, the vehicles just stood like parked cars, in hopeless silence, their drivers having given up and given in to the whims of the city's traffic flow.

There was a honk from behind the son. He spun around, a little startled by the unexpected direction from where the sound came. It was the ambulance driver motioning him to step out of the vehicle's way. The ambulance could move only a few feet forward and then it too came to a dead stop, rammed head-to-head with the unmoving traffic.

The son stood around stupidly, next to the ambulance. What was he expecting? He couldn't tell. Maybe some deus ex machina chopper to airlift him out of this gridlock.

'Behenchod, this traffic has made mother and sister one!' the ambulance driver remarked to his sidekick. The driver's mouth was red with paan—a sign that his day had ended, and now some highs were in order. The assistant acknowledged the comment with a nod; he was talking on his cell phone.

The son glanced in their direction. He did a double-take at the blue beacon above the driver's cabin.

'I need to get to Breach Candy Hospital,' the son said to the driver. 'Urgently! Can you take me?'

The driver seemed taken aback by the request. He tried to make sense of it: 'Breach Candy? But I picked you up from Jaslok. Why would you want to go anywhere right now? Don't you want to bury your father first?'

A decade ago, when he had just returned from his studies in New York, the dead man's son would have been outraged by the man's presumptuousness. Now he was used to the Indian penchant for trying to figure out other people's business. The dead man's son had begun doing it too—thinking and plotting several steps ahead, assuming everyone else to be an imbecile.

'My wife is about to give birth,' the dead man's son said. 'Please!'

The driver's assistant had hung up by then. He heard the news and both he and the ambulance driver hooted loudly. 'What life does!' the driver exclaimed. 'What life does sometimes!'

'Please, I need to get to Breach Candy right away!'

The driver shook his head in disbelief. 'We are not allowed to ferry passengers, saab. Only the sick or dead...'

The driver looked like he needed a figure. The dead man's son ventured one.

They finally settled on an amount three times more than what the son had paid to transport his father's body to the kabrastan. The assistant was packed into the back of the ambulance; he was told to lie down on one of the planks to deflect any police scrutiny.

The son hopped in next to the driver. The driver flicked a silver switch on the dashboard. The ambulance siren came on. The son could see the blue beacon flashing on things around them as it turned and turned. The siren started to work its magic. Motorists switched the ignitions of their vehicles on. They began changing gears and inching their vehicles—forward, sideways, anywhere they saw a gap—in an attempt to make way for the emergency vehicle.

'Munnu, you remain sleeping!' the driver yelled towards the back of the ambulance. He looked at the dead man's son. 'I am taking risk, saab, very big risk.'

The siren was worsening an already chaotic traffic situation.

Drivers were doing whatever they could to scramble out of the way.

The dead man's son was witness to a side of the city he didn't know existed. Or maybe it was an aspect that he had never seen until now—the unthinking responsiveness to someone else's hour of need.

A path began to clear for the ambulance; it was allowed to wind its way past vehicles that had been log-jammed for tens of minutes. The son glanced at the side-view mirror. He chuckled. As soon as their ambulance passed, the traffic closed in again, congealed in a matter of seconds, a stalemate of egos and automobiles.

The dead man's grandson was born at 5.39 p.m. Precisely seventeen minutes after his grandfather was buried in the Shia Imami Ismaili Kabrastan in Dongri.

The dead man's son could witness neither event. On the bridge leading to Tardeo Junction, roughly halfway between the graveyard and the hospital, the ambulance the dead man's son was travelling in found itself in the middle of a traffic deadlock of mammoth proportions. The jam would be written about in the next day's papers. Hundreds of people missed their flights. Thousands of people were late for important appointments. Tens of thousands of frantic phone calls, posts and tweets were made from cell phones along the congested route. Someone's sister had committed suicide. Someone's building had collapsed. Someone's brother had been found murdered by the domestic help. The city's unforgiving traffic refused to make way, heedless of the urgency.

The dead man's son abandoned the ambulance and began walking. By the time he reached the hospital, his wife was in a post-delivery daze in her private room, his newborn son was in custody of the nurses, and he learnt over a phone call with his mother that one of his father's brothers had become uncontrollable the moment the gravediggers lowered the corpse into the ground. The dead man's son realized he had been wrong. The dead man did have it in him to invoke hysteria in others.

The dead man's son lay down on the visitor's sofa in the hospital room. He dozed. He dreamt of his father. He heard an infant crying at the far end of the corridor of the maternity ward. The sound came closer. His wife stirred. Closer. Closer. There was a knock on the door.

As he rushed to take possession of the bundled being bawling in the nurse's arms, the dead man's son reverted to his old dissociative trick. He thought about how, at that precise moment, there were probably thousands of fathers across the country holding their newborns for the first time. It didn't work. Placing himself in the context of a larger mass of humanity did nothing to lessen the immediate, tactile bliss of feeling his offspring's flesh and bones for the first time. The dead man's son passed the newborn into his mother's eager embrace. He sat back on the visitor's sofa. He imagined being buried in place of his father under several feet of graveyard soil. The hospital room exploded with a vividness that was unbearable. With the son under the kabrastan, the dead man was free to be here, in this sea-facing hospital room, sitting on the visitor's sofa in place of his son, watching his grandson squirm against the cloth constricting his limbs. The dead man's son jumped up and joined his wife on her hospital bed. The dead man's son kissed his son's head. He touched his son's tiny nose and traced his tiny jaw. He breathed in the smell of the newborn's just washed hair. He took it all in with the relish of a dead man brought back to life.

MmYum's

Of Camel Backs and Last Straws

HE feels empty. Hollow. Unreal. He feels he has no business being alive. He hopes his sentience is a flash in the pan. He keeps sitting. And waiting. And watching. And waiting. But his consciousness refuses to fade. He tries his best not to move. He struggles to maintain the position in which he'd come alive: arms outstretched on the top edge of the wooden bench, his green boots crossed casually. He doesn't slacken his hysterical smile, never lets tiredness or irritation creep into his overexcited expression.

As days turn to nights, the ebb and flow of customers continue unabated all around him in the alfresco section of the chain store's downtown Mumbai branch. No one knows that he is alive, that he is watching them. He sees people eating and chatting, laughing and arguing. He endures the punches of kids and the occasional shock of scalding hot coffee being dropped on his shoulder or head. Thank goodness he is made of plasto-plastic. The alfresco section hosts birthday parties and office get-togethers. He is always the centre of attraction. Sometimes young actors sit on either side of him on the bench and practise their dialogues. Over weeks and weeks of watching, he finds himself falling in love with people. The young and the old, the men and women and children. The middle class, the wealthy, the ugly, the breathtaking, the fat, the thin. He adores them all.

When night falls and the restaurant closes, it is just him and the pot-head watchman who lolls about on the footpath smoking joints and having quickies with whores.

He gets up from his bench in the dark. He stretches his acrylic limbs. He ventures to the far edge of the alfresco section and peeks out through the potted plants. He sees trees, cars and a handful of people still milling around even at this time of the night. Sometimes he catches sight of the moon.

He tries to enter the main restaurant. But the place is always sealed, the glass doors always locked. Through the full-length windows he sees the counter glowing dimly under the half-lit overhead lights. He gazes at the huge menu board with its tantalizing photos of the food people come here to eat. He returns to his bench and lies down.

He knows who he is. He doesn't know why he is alive. He knows what he is called and what is expected of him. He doesn't know for how long he can continue like this, pretending to be unfeeling and unseeing, when all he wants is to walk around and yak non-stop like everyone else.

He hopes he can find the forbearance to keep up the mascot-clown act. He hopes he doesn't snap one day and decide he's had enough. As dawn approaches, he returns to his bench, to his original lounging pose. By the time the day's first delivery happens at 6 a.m., he has grown as still as the tables and chairs around him.

The Kurta-pyjamafication of Arnold MmYum

It happens on a steaming May evening. While the staff at MmYum's downtown Mumbai branch is busy festooning the alfresco section in preparation for yet another brat's birthday party, the chain store's mascot-clown decides he's had enough. To hell with his Protestant work ethic. He could no longer endure the tropical heat, the din of traffic, or the prospect of being molested by yet another horde of monstrous pre-teens.

Arnold gets up from his bench. He shrugs off the terrified six-year-old clinging to his leg and walks out of the restaurant. Two watchmen give chase. Arnold hides behind a garbage dump near Sterling Cinema until it is dark.

Over subsequent days, as Arnold flits about Mumbai's streets, he is assailed by prostitutes, gigolos, beggars and drug peddlers. Opportunistic taxi drivers begin to trail the mascot, assuming him to be a lost tourist. MmYum's-fed children recognize Arnold and insist—to the international mascot's horror and to their parents' acute embarrassment—on playing with 'clown uncle'.

Arnold wishes he could be less noticeable. His multicoloured body parts had been spray-painted onto his plasto-plastic frame, intrinsic as a human's skin. For some fortuitous reason, Arnold's creator had fashioned the clown's lips out of soft rubber, enabling him to close his grinning mouth. In all other aspects, Arnold considered himself cursed by his unknown creator.

Arnold becomes convinced that half his troubles would vanish if he concealed his lurid clown body. His panic-stricken meandering through the city narrows down to a frantic search for disguise. The clown observes people gifting food and money to beggars. No one offered the destitute clothing. Since free clothes were out of the question, Arnold tries to filch garments left to dry on washing lines outside ground-floor flats. After a few close shaves with screechy housewives and alert watchmen, the clown gives up on this dangerous option. Eventually, in keeping with his corporate antecedents, Arnold clothes himself by robbing a farmer.

From among scores of people who take shelter on the concourse of CST station one rainy night, the Maharashtrian farmer befriends only Arnold. When the agriculturalist returns from the washroom, he finds that the tall and clownish white gentleman whom he'd entrusted with his belongings had disappeared with his bag containing four pairs of kurta-pyjamas, three raw-silk turban cloths, and twenty thousand rupees in hard cash. (Somewhere in the interiors of Vidarbha is a grieving cotton grower who has been cured at long last of his colonial hangover.)

Arnold was lucky to have burgled a man as tall and big-boned as himself. It takes a little practice getting the turban around his head, but the clothes fit to a T.

And the cash from the farmer's bag? Bribe for a posse of policemen to overlook Arnold's non-possession of ID proof or residency documents.

And the bag and the rest of the farmer's belongings? Mugged by a gang of beggars in a savage early morning attack, which leaves Arnold with the clothes on his back, a chipped skull and knees and a crushed will.

Before running away from MmYum's, Arnold spent several weeks watching people and their ways in the world. He wondered what it was like to be one of them, to be part of life's thrumming, fast-paced symphony.

What seemed intriguing from the bench of a fast-food restaurant turns out to be a violent and survivalist nightmare up close. After spending several days and nights on Mumbai's streets, being hounded by dogs, policemen and gangsters, Arnold realizes that he was better off at MmYum's, better off faking lifelessness for the enjoyment of cruel children and perverted adults. Real life was too difficult. Arnold didn't want to be one among humans, he didn't want his freedom. All said and done, Arnold preferred to just sit and stare.

The mascot-clown winds his way back to his home branch in downtown Mumbai, hoping to resume his bench duty. He is in for a shock. Sprawled on the bench in MmYum's open-air dining section is Arnold's replica. The truant Arnold MmYum had been replaced by a new one. Desperate, Arnold dumps his farmer's garb under the bench and sits down next to the new him. It isn't long before the branch manager comes and taps the prodigal on the shoulder.

Arnold begs to be reinstated. The manager refuses. 'You should have thought twice before running away like that. We couldn't wait for you forever. Business was suffering.' Allowing two mascots to serve at the same premises was against MmYum's store policy. While putting on his farmer's clothes, Arnold notices something that tells him everything he needs to know about MmYum's and its capitalist workings: The new Arnold, still lifeless by all indications, had been fastened to the bench and floor with six-inch screws that had been driven in through the backs of his palms and into his feet.

Arnold begins hanging around at MmYum's. Despite the crucifixion of his replacement, the stranded mascot-clown yearned to be reabsorbed into MmYum's empire. Anything was better than being stuck on these savage Developing World streets filled with brown people and mangy dogs. Maybe there was a new outlet somewhere in need of a mascot? The branch manager promises to let Arnold know.

While his days are spent lurking in and around the secure confines of the restaurant, Arnold's street-side nights are still stalked by threats of crime and violence. Now all he needs is some place safe to spend the nights.

Arnold tries to befriend ordinary people, the ones who come to eat at MmYum's and the ones who work there, in the hope that one of them might take pity and provide the mascot-clown with temporary shelter.

Employees at the downtown Mumbai branch had been advised to offer no assistance to the breakaway mascot. MmYum's head office was in the process of investigating whether a rival chain store might be trying to lure Arnold away. It was also possible that the sentient Arnold was in fact a real person in the mascot-clown's costume, an activist of some anti-American non-profit organization out to ridicule the international chain store.

Arnold doesn't have much luck with the customers either. Ordinary folks are creeped out by the sight of a mascot-clown dressed in an Indian farmer's costume of soiled kurta-pyjama and crumpled turban. Multinational businesses were renowned for their misguided marketing campaigns in India. Putting Arnold into a farmer's clothes was only slightly less offensive than wrapping a saree around a life-sized turkey, as some culturally insensitive international firm had recently done in New Delhi. Given the weirdness of his get-up, and coupled with his alienating New York accent, Arnold fails to insinuate himself with the locals. Foreign backpackers, who might have empathized with Arnold's roofless condition, were nowhere in sight. It was still the peak of summer, a time when no sensible melanin-challenged westerner dared to venture anywhere near the sizzling subcontinent.

It would take that rare sort of person, with an offbeat

sense of humour and a refined political sensibility, to grasp the incredible irony of an international mascot-clown coming alive and becoming marooned on the streets of a post-colonial Asian city. Unfortunately for Arnold, those rare sorts of people usually stayed miles away from mass-market chain stores like MmYum's.

The operative term being 'usually'.

American junk food has a lure that not even the most passionate anti-capitalist can resist. One taste of onion rings, one sip of cola, or one sampling of a mayonnaise-doused deep-fried chicken cutlet is enough to infect one with a lifelong craving for these so-called foods. The fence-sitters have it worst—the ones who embrace the spoils of free markets while being simultaneously revolted by the joy they derive from roaming in malls, working for foreign companies, wearing Western brands and surreptitiously gorging on Western junk food. Lacking both the moral rigour of radicals and the blissful indifference of the masses, these guilt-ridden fence-sitters are destined to lives of paralysing shame and unbounded wantonness.

It had been weeks since Unnati Lodha went to MmYum's. The last time she ate there, she swore never to come back. By week four of abstinence, however, Unnati could feel her will weaken. The ideological barriers in her brains stood no chance against the craving in her blood. Her anti-globalization opinions could go to hell. Unnati had to have her Yuma burger with o-rings and icy, gassy cola. Yes. Yes! Nothing else will do.

Skipping the blah lunch her mother has prepared, Unnati rushes out. It is an ultra-mega-humid June afternoon. It takes Unnati half an hour to reach downtown Mumbai. She breathes easier on seeing the MmYum's logo looming over the crowded footpath.

Unnati is welcomed to MmYum's. Would she like to try the… No, no, she just wants the usual. Money, change, fast, now!

When the YumYuma meal is served, Unnati grabs the tray and carries it off like a jungle animal afraid to share. Her usual corner seat at the back is occupied by an amorous couple taking full advantage of the privacy. Too impatient to care about being spotted at MmYum's neo-colonial feeding ground, Unnati plonks down at a street-facing table, tears open the packaging, and sinks her teeth into clouds of carbohydrous pleasure.

Ooohhh, she goes.

Mmmmm.

And then… Eeeek!

On the other side of the window, waving to get her attention, is a tall, weirdly built and unnaturally white-skinned man dressed in a kurta-pyjama, with a turban on his funny-shaped head.

Is it…?

It is. Dressed like a Maharashtrian cotton grower, it is Arnold MmYum the clown!

Unnati stops chewing and watches with bewilderment as the world-famous MmYum's mascot tries to mime something to her through the soundproof window. Being a struggling novelist, she knows all about allegories, and how to behave when one has unwittingly become part of one.

Unnati shrugs to express her inability to understand what Arnold is saying. He motions her to hang on, he will join her, and then he disappears from her field of vision.

Here we go, Unnati mutters under her breath. She gobbles up the rest of her burger and sucks up the remaining cola. By the time Arnold lumbers up to her table half a minute later, Unnati's tray is a wasteland of paper packaging and ketchup-stained tissues.

'Hello, there,' the clown says.

'Hello?' Unnati looks up with scepticism.

'I'm Arnold MmYum, mascot-clown of this wonderfu...'

'I know who you are.'

'Mind if I join you?' the clown asks.

'Yes, I do.'

'Hahaha!' The clown lets out an embarrassed chuckle. 'Hahaha!'

Unnati decides to go easy on the poor chap. 'Sit.' She points to the empty chair across the table.

Owing to his abnormally long torso, Arnold looks like he is standing even when seated. He slouches over the table, unsure of where to place his unusually long hands.

'What can I do for you?' Unnati asks. She sits back in her seat and places one leg over another.

'You must be dumbfounded to see me,' Arnold says. 'I mean, it's me!'

Unnati feigns indifference. 'It's an allegory, all sorts of things can happen in allegories. I don't mind playing along...'

Arnold has a good feeling about this woman. She speaks like no one else he's met. 'You come here often? To eat? Miss... uh...?'

'Wow, it's been a long time since someone called me Miss,' she says, popping a stray piece of onion ring into her mouth. 'I'm Unnati. And no, I don't come here often.'

'Because I haven't seen you before. I mean, I would've noticed you. A striking lady like you is hard to miss.'

Unnati smiles. 'Oh really?' She imagines intercourse with the clown. Her well-manicured toes curl in repulsion.

Arnold decides to cut to the chase. He was tired of the introductory small talk. Unnati was the seventh customer he had approached since morning. What two-faced bastards these Indians were. They all told Arnold how much they loved MmYum's and how much they adored the mascot-clown. But when it came to taking the clown home, they all came up with the most ludicrous excuses.

Oh, I'm sorry, Arnold, my home is being renovated.

Or, *I have relatives visiting from abroad.*

Or, *I don't have a home either, Arnold, I'm just like you.*

The clown cursed the day he'd run away from his bench.

'Do you live close by?' Arnold asks. Before Unnati can answer, the clown blurts out his real intentions: 'Can you take me home? I don't have any place to live. I just need some place safe to spend the nights, just temporarily, until I'm assigned a bench at another MmYum's branch...' Arnold trails off. He adjusts the turban on his massive head and gazes at Unnati's expressionless face for some sign of willingness.

Unnati fiddles with an unused packet of ketchup on her tray. This was interesting. Sitting across from her inside the faux-festive premises of MmYum's was the very icon of neo-liberal globalization, begging for shelter.

'Is this a joke?'

Arnold shakes his head. 'I'm for real, Unnati. I mean, as real as someone like me can get. I really need a place to live. I'm desperate!'

Unnati feels sorry for the clown. He couldn't have approached a more dangerous person for assistance. 'I can't take you home,' she says. The clown continues to stare at her. 'I live with my parents. They wouldn't approve if I brought home male company. You are male, aren't you?' Arnold tries to blubber out a response. Unnati continues: 'Anyway, it doesn't matter. Women don't do such things in India. We can't just pick up strangers and take them home. Not yet, at least.'

Arnold gazes out of the window. 'I understand. I'm, I'm sorry, I'm still trying to understand the culture.'

'But...'

Arnold jerks his head back in Unnati's direction.

'I have a friend. He might be able to.'

Arnold nods his head.

'Give me a sec,' Unnati says. 'Let me see what I can do.' She excuses herself to make a phone call.

Arnold watches her go, his eyes lingering on Unnati's bottom without understanding why. He is overwhelmed by the woman's generosity. If being a man means being with someone like Unnati, Arnold suddenly has an aching desire to be one, to become human.

Unnati takes long, but she returns smiling. 'It's done. I spoke to my friend; he said you can crash at his place for as long as you need.'

It was physiologically impossible for Arnold to weep, or even frown, or widen his eyes and laugh. Without the props of expressions, his profuse thank-yous have a ring of insincerity to them. It makes Unnati feel a little less guilty for what she was doing to him. 'I'll drop you off at Aftab's on my way home. Right away. Shall we?'

On his way out, Arnold informs the branch manager about his stroke of good luck. The manager glances at Unnati as she waits on the footpath. 'I don't have a good feeling about this, Arnold,' the manager confides. 'Take care of yourself. Try to check in here every day. There might be an opening for you soon.'

Arnold cannot contain his excitement. It was his first ever taxi ride, his first foray into the innards of the city. He looks at everything from the vehicle's window. A perky clueless newly sentient mascot-clown being driven to the gallows.

After what seems like an interminable detour through a badly maintained city landscape, Unnati orders the cab driver to stop at the gate of a freshly painted building. The mascot-clown peers out of the window at their destination.

'This is where Aftab lives,' Unnati says. 'Go up, Arnold. They're waiting for you.'

Arnold asks, 'Aren't you coming along?'

'No, sweety, I have a novel to finish.'

The clown gets out of the cab and leans in to wave goodbye.

'Flat 903, ninth floor. Take care, my dear.' Unnati blows a kiss at him.

It is the last the clown will see of her for a very long time.

As the taxi zooms away, Arnold is puzzled. Did Unnati say 'they'?

Arnold MmYum Makes New Friends

Unnati would have liked to escort Arnold up to Aftab's flat. But she had been prohibited from doing so. By pigging out at MmYum's, Unnati had forfeited the right to be among the proactive and politically aware citizens who would be awaiting Arnold's arrival at Aftab's home.

Aftab had minced no words on the phone. Who was Unnati? As a woman—exceptionally beautiful and sharp. As a writer—unpublished and untested. And as a citizen? The less said the better. Someone who still lived with her parents, who obviously had no control over her dietary urges and had never ordered a gas cylinder or visited a police station, such a person hardly deserved to be involved in the process of undermining a global economic system. Unnati just happened to be in the right place, thanks to her incurable addiction to MmYum's pap. For the sake of the nation, she would have to surrender Arnold into better hands. A dispossessed multinational mascot-clown needed to be surrounded by only the most committed and ruthless minds. Aftab was sorry to say Unnati just doesn't cut it.

The eleven who do make the cut receive an all-caps group-SMS from Aftab seconds after he has got off the phone with Unnati:

DROP EVRYTHNG & B @ MY PLACE ASAP! MESSIAH ON THE WAY!

And so they come, dropping everything, excusing themselves from work, requesting friends or neighbours to babysit their kids, walking out of cinema halls and bookshops and leaving half-finished glasses of beer on the tables of their favourite watering holes. One by one or in twos, they converge from disparate parts of town: Kandivali, Worli, Versova, Ballard Estate... The time warp of city commuting ensures that regardless of how far they've come from, the chosen eleven reach Aftab's at roughly the same time.

The 'messiah' was yet to arrive. Refusing to give any clues, Aftab stomps around his home gleefully and serves tea to his amused guests.

Half past four in the afternoon. The bell rings.

'Must be him!'

They all gather at the door.

Aftab peers through the peephole. He wails, 'Noooo...!'

What? What?

'He's not what I expected. Brace yourselves, people!'

Aftab opens the door.

Standing on the coir foot mat, holding his palms up in an awkward namaste...

'It's Arnold MmYum, ladies and gentleman! Dressed like a...' Aftab blinks his eyes for effect, 'like a Marathwada yokel, I believe.'

On the morning Arnold was attacked by the beggars, he was lying in Azad Maidan with the Maharashtrian farmer's suitcase under his head. He had spent the entire night staring at the stars. Unable to blank out the world visually (since his eyes are moulded open), Arnold has learnt to cover his field of vision with dreaminess, so that during the few hours that he 'sleeps', the things he sees blur into visions of his slumber. When he saw the leering unkempt faces of the beggar brigade looking down at him against the backdrop of a dawn sky, the sight was so improbable and terrifying, Arnold thought he was having the first real nightmare of his wakeful sleep. A kick to his head told him the nine beggars were all too real. Browned as they were by dirt, it was hard to tell their ages or sexes. Arnold curled up and endured their punches. No one came to his rescue. Having no skin or internal organs, Arnold experienced the beating like the impacts of sonic booms. It was the jolt to his non-existent heart that was most excruciating—the dismay at being on the receiving end of arbitrary and unprovoked savagery.

And now it was happening all over again. Sitting on a cane chair in Aftab's living room, looking from one bloodthirsty face to another, Arnold wonders if he wasn't better off on the streets. To encounter the savagery of the footpath in a homely ninth-floor flat was beyond horrifying. Where was Unnati? Did she know what was being done to him?

As soon as Arnold sits down, the twelve radicals, Aftab included, begin to heap the clown with abuses, insults and accusations. You neo-liberal thug, you neo-colonial murderer, you stooge of capitalist greed, you shitty symbol of puerile global merchandising... All twelve speak at once, their vicious hate-filled words directed solely at the dazed mascot-clown. Take off this kurta-pyjama, how dare you mock a nation's garb. Take of that turban—the symbol of a rural man's respectability. What does a mascot-clown know about respectability? Or simplicity? All Arnold knows is greed. More, more, more fast-food outlets in more countries to junk up as many stomachs as possible. You bastard motherfucker randi kutta chutiya sala sooar... One of Aftab's invitees goes out of control and has to be taken to another room. Thrash him, a white-haired woman in a cotton saree demands, smash Arnold's skull the way they do it to villagers trying to protect their lands against dams and international airports. Diabetes, cancer, consumerism, poverty, global warming, air pollution, water pollution, avarice, promiscuity, vices, Arnold is accused of all these. And more: discontent, destitution, disease, and death. No, Arnold wants to say, no, no...

'Kill him, I want to kill the clown!' the out-of-control man returns from the other room and has to be restrained by the others. Two men direct some of their rage at Aftab. You should have warned us, Aftab, this is no joke, we would have come prepared with photos and documents to leave this clown with no doubt about his masters' destructive deeds. Others agree; Aftab should have let them know. Some 'messiah' this. Heartless clown, says a woman, knocking on Arnold's chest. See, hollow, just as I expected. They go on for more than an hour. A young bald man sits on the floor at Arnold's feet. He has the coldest eyes Arnold has seen in a human being. The man's whispering is more terrifying than the shouting and yelling. Our nation is dying because of your influence, do you know that? We will not let you put price tags on our water, our very air. We don't need air conditioning; we don't need malls, skyscrapers, SUVs, or that fatty sugary stomach-fucking shit that you peddle at MmYum's. Please, *please*, LEAVE US THE FUCK ALONE!

Arnold curls up on the cane chair as if in preparation for yet another thrashing. He hunches his shoulders, buries his face in his knees and lets out an injured whine. *Please, please don't hit me, please, please don't hit me...*

His tormentors exhale. Their job was done. Having reduced the world-famous Arnold MmYum to the equivalent of an oppressed farmer snivelling for mercy from a brutal police force, Aftab and his invitees had notched a small but significant triumph against financial fascism. Now there was nothing Arnold couldn't be made to do. It makes Aftab's gang giddy imagining all the farmer uprisings, labour unions, environmental groups and social justice missions that could win victory upon victory by the mere presence among them of a sympathetic ex-multinational mascot.

No, please, please don't hit me, please...

A temporarily deranged Arnold is led to the bedroom and made to lie down. He is left alone. He curls up again, trembling, cowering to protect himself and begging to be spared.

Once he is convinced that no harm will come to him, that no overexcited madman will yet again storm into the room baying for his head, Arnold calms down. He sits up on the bed and proceeds, in the venerable tradition of sentience, to reflect upon his condition.

Despite the horror of what he had just endured, Arnold was relieved to discover that he wasn't some causeless random accident of dummy manufacturing. While the origin of his consciousness was as yet a mystery, it was clear, from the way those people out there were ready to tear him apart, that something had preceded Arnold, something that was immense and destructive and so closely connected to him that, whether or not it was fair, he was being held accountable for transgressions that weren't his own. Poverty, pollution, farmer suicides, gas leaks… Arnold had been accused of things he had no recollection of. Painfully, tragically, his wish to be part of the human world was finally coming true. He was being sucked in, even if it was as an enemy. After stumbling about the streets for weeks mattering to no one, Arnold was thankful to be among people who felt so strongly about him.

He hears them arguing. He sees the light filter in through the bottom of the bedroom door. Arnold gets up. It is dusk; the room is almost dark. His turban is a messy heap on the pillow. He has rid himself of the kurta-pyjama. Hoping to rejoin his rude hosts, Arnold tries the door knob.

He is overjoyed to find the door locked from outside. It meant Aftab and his friends didn't want Arnold to go anywhere. It meant Arnold was expected to be nowhere but here.

Arnold sits on the edge of the bed and places his hands on his knees. He sets his eyes on the door, anxious to know what's in store.

Three a.m., and the stalemate in Aftab's living room continues. After hours of trying to convince each other, the twelve still couldn't agree over what to do with the clown.

Odisha, Gujarat, Chhattisgarh, Kerala, Manipur, Arunachal Pradesh, Punjab, the interiors of Maharashtra itself… there wasn't a state or a district in the entire nation where citizens weren't marching, rioting, fasting, suing, lobbying, voting, boycotting or committing suicide to voice their feeble and pathetic protests against the tightening stranglehold of multinational corporations.

If it wasn't the firms themselves, it was the government acting on their behalf—linking rivers, charting expressways, stacking up dams and cranking up polluting power plants amid ancient fruit-producing backwoods.

The surprising thing, Aftab and his friends conclude, isn't that Arnold MmYum had come alive, but that, from among hundreds of mascots vegetating in fast-food chains across the country, only this one had deigned to show up.

Each person in Aftab's living room pushes a different agenda for Arnold. While someone wants him to address a fishermen's rally in Sardham, someone else thinks he should infiltrate AMERCA and create havoc in the Fortune 500 Company. Maybe, Aftab suggests, Arnold MmYum could become the world's first anti-brand, representing nothing, selling nothing. Or maybe, someone else pipes up, Arnold could establish an ashram, and MmYumDham could have residents from the world over living out a post-consumerist utopia.

But what about the caste system, couldn't Arnold do something about that? And what about the Hindu–Muslim problem? And the Bihari–Marathi feud? Wait a minute! *What about Kashmir!*

On and on they go. In trying to outdo each other, their visions for Arnold's destiny grow more outrageous by the hour.

Arnold should be a politician. No, he should become a militant. No, he should be an all-purpose activist. No, he should cycle across the globe extolling the virtues of environmentalism.

The frizzy-haired woman who knocked on Arnold's chest wonders if they weren't being awfully proprietary about the clown. Considering it was his fate on the line, shouldn't Arnold be part of the discussion too?

'Enough!' It is quarter to four in the morning. Aftab has had enough. He waves dismissively at the main door, kept ajar for ventilation. 'Everybody out. You're all useless. History has dealt us a trump card, and this is how we play our hand? Like bickering schoolgirls? All of you just get lost! I'll decide about Arnold myself!'

No one budges. Instead, they fix Aftab with amused beleaguered stares. These were seasoned players, adept at browbeating state ministers, pushing through police barricades and mocking judicial diktats. Not nobodies to be ordered around like peons.

The woman in the saree speaks up. 'You are going to do no such thing, my dear Aftab. Arnold's presence is of national concern. If we can't agree about him, we'd rather throw him out than let you decide by yourself.'

Aftab looks around the room.

The others shrug, nod and pout to express their agreement with the woman in the saree. (Later they will say they were too tired and sleepy and weren't thinking clearly.)

'Fine then!' Aftab gets to his feet, meaning to call their bluff.

His guests groan.

He marches to the bedroom door and unlocks it. Arnold squeals as Aftab drags him out into the hall.

'Arnold is going to start his own Madras Café chain, and we are going to help him!' This was Aftab's latest brainwave, one which he was utterly convinced about.

'Over our dead bodies,' says a man.

Snorts and chortles erupt in the room.

Aftab pushes Arnold towards the wide open main door. 'You can get lost, Arnold. I'm sorry, but we don't know what to do with you. Remember to tell people how close you were to history's centre stage...'

'And also!' the icy-eyed bald man adds, 'tell people how this roomful of bumbling clowns let you down!'

Now the laughter cannot be controlled.

'Please,' Arnold says, 'I have nowhere to go. I'll do anything you all want. Please, please let me stay here, please!'

'Sorry, Arnold,' the saree-clad woman literally shrieks with mirth, 'your host has spoken. It's the highway for you!'

Incensed by the mockery, Aftab jostles a pleading Arnold out into the lobby. 'Just fuck off!' He shuts the door on Arnold.

Exactly ten hours after he rang Aftab's bell, Arnold is back where he started.

Aftab swaggers back to his armchair. With Arnold actually out of the flat, the situation has been drained of hilarity.

All twelve sit in silence.

Five minutes pass.

'He said he'd do anything for us,' the frizzy-haired woman comments.

All twelve jump to their feet. They dash for the door. It no longer matters what each of them wanted for Arnold. Right now, all they want is to get Arnold back.

The landing was empty.

The elevator was still on the floor.

'He must have taken the stairs!'

Four people start running down the stairs. Six others, Aftab included, crowd into the tiny elevator. The night had turned into a thriller.

The lift group and the staircase group reach the ground floor at roughly the same time. They dash around the foyer looking for Arnold.

They run to the gate. The side gate is open. The watchman is caught dozing. 'I swear, madam, no one left the gate! I swear, sir, no one has gone out!' But there was no way to be sure.

They rush out to the street. They look this way and that.

How could Arnold have gone so far so soon? How was it possible?

Defeated and bewildered, the ten take the elevator back to the ninth floor in two lots.

'Where is he?' the two women who had stayed behind in Aftab's flat ask. 'Where is the clown?'

The ten who went looking for him have no idea. Arnold, it seems, had disappeared the way he had appeared: a prank of the city's roguish, muggy air.

It's Raining Clowns

Arnold has never been this high. He is on the wind-blown terrace of Aftab's eleven-storey building. Despite being far above the unpopulated night-time streets, the city looked no less menacing to the clown.

Arnold approaches the edge of the terrace. His orange hands tremble as he places them on the ledge. He looks over. Down below, in the compound surrounding the building, the parked cars look like insects swarming around a tree.

Darkened skyscrapers of varying heights and shapes were visible all around. The deserted street twisted and turned and then disappeared into a sharp left turn. From this height, it was impossible not to gain perspective. As Arnold looks from end to end of the city, he grows increasingly gloomy about his prospects of surviving here.

To be back-stabbed by women posing as friends, to be humiliated and assaulted and accused of things he didn't even do, is this why he had come alive? The thought of descending this building and returning to the real world drains Arnold. He sits down. He wishes he could hide up here forever. But it will be morning soon. The two old handymen whom Arnold had stepped over to enter the terrace will surely have him thrown out when they wake up and discover him. That's what people do. They are violent and wicked and, like Aftab, they expel you without warning or explanation.

A plane passes noiselessly overhead. Arnold gazes at the night sky. So many clouds. And inside his hollow head, within his non-existent brain, so many questions. Why him? Why him alive? How does he know to speak? And why English of all human languages?

Like an astronaut locked away permanently inside his body-shaped space suit, Arnold experiences the usual human appetites and sensations, but lacks the means to relieve himself. Why this hunger in him if there was no stomach to fill? Why did he feel itchy without a skin to scratch? Why this incessant, unrelenting suffering?

Arnold raises his acrylic hulk and peers over the ledge once again. A truck was racing down the street from the left. A bus was approaching from the opposite side. Two leviathans hurtling towards each other. Arnold's attention is drawn to the horizon, where the glow from an industrial complex had reddened the night sky.

Exactly two floors below, at roughly the same spot, Aftab was at his window looking out at the same view, ashamed to turn around and face his friends as they start to leave. He watches a bus and truck swerve past each other without incident. He wonders how long it will take for this night to be forgotten and for his guilt to ebb.

'Bye, Aftab.'

'Chal, see ya, man.'

'Good night, Aftab.'

Where did that bloody clown go?

It is close to five in the morning by the time everyone leaves. Aftab sits by the window in the dark, unable to sleep. As punishment for losing Arnold and letting the nation down, he considers killing himself. Only Arnold, with his American accent and Caucasian poise, could have dinned anti-materialist sense into Westoxicated Indians. With Arnold gone, there was no way to counter the ravages of so-called development being mandated by greedy outsiders in collusion with the starry-eyed natives themselves.

Aftab clutches the window sill. He imagines leaping out and crashing onto the concrete road below. Even death was preferable to witnessing the gradual ruination of this precious, beloved land.

Whoooppp...

As if like a dummy run of his own fall, a dark bulk whooshes past Aftab's window.

Aftab's first instinct is to jump back. He sticks his head out gingerly and sees Arnold descending towards the road, the clown's multicoloured arms and legs flailing wildly in the dark.

Aftab's horror turns into astonishment when he realizes that Arnold's velocity was less than that of an average falling object. Maybe it had something to do with the hollowness of Arnold's plasto-plastic mass, or maybe it was due to the inflexibility of his body surface. Whatever it was, gravity had let the clown off easy.

Arnold lands on the street face-down with a loud thump. The sound disturbs a couple of beggars sleeping nearby. They raise their heads. Finding nothing unremarkable about a life-sized clown lying on the footpath, they smack their lips and go back to sleep. By then, Aftab was practically flying down the stairs of his building, bounding over entire flights in a couple of reckless dangerous leaps.

He throws himself over the last flight and tears across the foyer. The din of Aftab's approaching footsteps startles the dozing watchman. He dives out of the way, allowing Aftab to run unhindered through the parking lot and out of the side gate.

Aftab runs to the end of the street. He turns right. He is now on the footpath in front of his building. Aftab runs several feet ahead. He is now at the exact spot where Arnold must have landed.

There was nothing there to indicate impact. No chipped paint, no plasto-plastic splinters. There was only the sickening certainty of having missed an opportunity yet again.

'Arnold! Arnold!' Aftab looks around desperately for the clown. The sleeping beggars raise their heads once again, awakened by this new disturbance. For the second time that night, Aftab had reached too late. For the second time that night, Arnold had vanished.

Aftab returns home. He sits at his window till daybreak.

Sometime at around 6 a.m., at the far end of the street, Aftab thinks he sees the figure of a tall, full-bodied person walking towards the Saat Rasta junction. The light is too dim to be able to make out any details. It could have been Arnold. Aftab isn't sure.

An Eventful Morning

Unnati's call rouses Aftab from an action-packed and protracted nightmare. He did not, as he'd feared, dream of clowns.

'How did it go?' Unnati asks. 'What have you decided about Arnold? What great things is he going to do?'

'What time is it?'

'It's 11 a.m. Were you still sleeping?'

Aftab wishes Unnati would hang up and disappear forever. What happened with Arnold was appalling enough; Unnati's smugness would make Aftab want to jump out as well.

'Unnati, I don't know where Arnold is. He ran away, he bolted on us at four in the morning. We went looking for him all over the building and in the street...' *But like donkeys we did not climb two floors above to the terrace, where Arnold was hiding all along. I watched him fall, Unnati, I saw him waft down to the road and then walk away into the night.*

Unnati is stunned. How does one manage to lose a six-foot-tall acrylic mascot-clown? After all the trouble she took and insults she tolerated, she couldn't believe that Aftab and his politically active cohorts had been so negligent with Arnold. 'What can I say, Aftab? Who am I? As a writer, untested and unpublished. And as a citizen, the less said the better...'

Aftab groans and disconnects the line.

He finds it impossible to fall asleep again. Now all Aftab sees when he closes his eyes are Arnolds plummeting past his window over and over. A waving Arnold, followed by a cartwheeling Arnold, followed by a frowning Arnold, followed by a spreadeagled Arnold, followed by a laughing Arnold, followed by a bicycling Arnold...

Aftab gets up from the living-room sofa in a cold sweat.

He drifts to the window. The street is now a noisy river of cars, buses, scooters and umbrella-topped pedestrians coursing unknowingly over the spot where a mascot-clown fell and survived only hours ago. Aftab draws the curtain to shut out the gloom of the monsoon sky.

On his way to the bathroom he peeks into the spare bedroom,

where Arnold lay the previous evening. He is surprised to see the clown's kurta-pyjama in a neat pile on the bed. The turban was still on the pillow, wrapped in the shape of Arnold's big green head.

Aftab picks up Arnold's cream-coloured nylon kurta gingerly with his fingertips. The garment gives off an odour of turpentine. He pulls out a plastic bag from under the bed and stuffs the kurta into it. He is about to do the same with the pyjama, when he feels a papery stiffness in one of its pockets. He fishes out a light-blue paper. It was a flier Arnold must have picked up from somewhere. *All concerned citizens. Please join us for a protest rally against the Amboi Port project. 22 June, Azad Maidan, Mumbai.* The event was three weeks away. The posters and signs were all over the city. Activists from APAPA (Amboi Port Affected People's Association) had been handing out these fliers at public places for weeks. Aftab rolls up the paper and tosses it out of the bedroom window. He didn't want to hear any more talk of social advocacy for a long time. He dumps Arnold's clothes into the trash can.

The bell rings. Aftab lets in the domestic servant—Ipta-bai, a sixty-eight-year-old, slum-dwelling Maharashtrian woman who had been cleaning homes for over five decades. She gets to work without a word. In Aftab's home, located in the armpit of a mammoth twenty-first-century city, it is the start of yet another run-of-the-mill feudal day.

Arnold did not jump. He was knocked off his feet by an abrupt and powerful gust of breeze. The mascot-clown tried to grab the ledge as he stumbled off the terrace. All he caught was a handful of air, like a goodbye gift from a randomly cruel world.

The clown tumbled face-down. He watched the floors slide by. Waiting for him like a wall at the end of his fall was the hard footpath.

Why, Arnold asked, and got no reply. Fifth floor, fourth floor, third floor, second… *Why, why, wh…*

Aftab may have lost Arnold, but Unnati knew where to find him. Despite the pesky rains, she sets off immediately for MmYum's downtown Mumbai branch—this time, not as a junk-addicted guilt-ridden writer, but as a concerned citizen who had decided to take matters in her own hands.

Aftab must've given Arnold hell; why else would Arnold want to run away from his home in the middle of the night. Unnati doesn't know what she could say or do to win back the clown's trust. Her mouth dries up when, at the end of the forty-minute cab ride, the MmYum's logo comes into view.

The MmYum's open-air section was closed to the public. It had been cordoned off by blue plastic sheets. Two watchmen had been posted at the entrance to prevent people from venturing behind the sheets. 'Sorry madam, closed for repairs.' Unnati cannot hear any knocking or banging. Whoever heard of repairs in the monsoon?

As a result of the alfresco section being closed, the main restaurant was unusually crowded with lunching executives and class-bunking college-goers. Unnati does a quick scan of the premises. No Arnold in sight.

She scouts the nooks and crannies of the place, hoping to spot a moping mascot-clown.

Someone calls out to her, 'Excuse me, miss?' Unnati sees the branch manager striding towards her. He ushers Unnati to an empty spot beside the counter. 'Where's Arnold?' the manager asks.

'I don't know,' Unnati says, keeping an eye on the entrance, 'I came here looking for him myself.'

The manager crosses his arms like a detective. 'He left with you yesterday evening. Where did you take him?'

'To a friend's flat. But he ran away from there.'

'Where? Where did he go?'

'I just told you I don't know,' Unnati snaps. 'Besides, why do you care? Until yesterday, you didn't care where he went. You just didn't want him here, right?'

'Madam, please, if you know where Arnold is, tell him to come back here. There's an opening for him.'

'Where is the opening?'

'Here,' the manager replies.

'You mean at this branch?'

The manager exhales and nods.

'Why? I thought your branch already had a mascot. What happened to your new Arnold MmYum?'

The manager groans. 'What happened to our new Arnold MmYum?' He raises his hands to his face and kneads his eyes. 'Come,' he says, 'come with me…'

Unnati follows the manager out of the restaurant. The two watchmen step aside to let them into the shrouded open-air section.

Tables and chairs had been stacked up around the mascot-clown's bench. The manager motions Unnati to look behind the fortress-like arrangement. She can hear the muffled moans and grunts of what sounds like a buried animal.

Unnati squeezes through a spot between two tables, almost toppling the chairs piled high on them.

'Careful!' the manager calls out. 'Not too close! Or he might go wild again.'

Unnati manages to reach the mascot's bench at the centre of the maze. Her blood runs cold. The new Arnold MmYum was looking directly at Unnati. A white cloth had been tied around the lower half of his face. The mascot-clown struggled to get up from the bench but was held back by the screws driven into the backs of his palms and through his feet. The clown gives the bench a vigorous shake. Unnati didn't need to hear him speak to know that he was blazing with rage. She gulps and backs away slowly.

The manager greets her with his arms crossed, a beleaguered expression on his tired face. 'Now you see?'

'When…?' Unnati was too shocked to frame proper sentences. 'When did this one…?'

'Yesterday evening,' the manager says, 'right after you left with the first Arnold. This one started screaming, telling us to remove the screws from his hands and feet. He abused some of our customers too. And then he made derogatory comments about MmYum's food…'

'What did he say?'

'He called it pap, junk and stomach-fucking shit. That's when we had to gag him with the cloth. Head office says there is no way we can let this second Arnold get away. Each clown costs us over a lakh of rupees to customize and install. The only way I can set this one free is if the first one comes back and takes his place. So, madam, I am asking you once again: where is Arnold?'

Arnold wonders if the manager has gone mad. *I'm right here, you dick-head, gagged up and nailed down on this bench! I'm right here,* he tries to scream. His voice emerges as a hoarse grunt. He can only make out snippets of the conversation between the manager and the woman.

The woman: 'It's not fair to the second Arnold… I don't know… How can you be… So you gag him?'

The manager: 'Bring him back… It wasn't your business… Where is the first Arnold?'

First Arnold? Second Arnold? As the manager and the woman continue to squabble like high-school sweethearts, things become clearer to the bench-bound clown. Another clown had come alive before him. The woman took that clown somewhere the previous evening, and now she didn't know where he is. It dawns on the second Arnold that he would not be released from the bench until the previous Arnold returned to take his place. The hopelessness of his situation drives the second Arnold into a wild panic. He yanks at the screws with all his might. He gives the bench a massive jolt. It only leads to more pain.

Something breaks inside the second Arnold. He just knows that the first clown was never going to return and now he, the second one, was going to be stuck here on this bench forever—alive, awake and trapped!

The woman: 'If I… him back… do you promise…?'

The manager: 'I promise…'

Arnold sinks into a deep funk. They could make all the promises they want. He knew there was no escape for him. The mascot-clown regrets coming alive. How he curses the previous Arnold for abandoning the bench. Above all, how he loathes the powers that be at MmYum's for conceiving of mascot-clowns.

Arnold's dead,' Aftab says, 'or whatever the mascot-clown equivalent of it is. Now please stop phoning me.'

'But you said…'

'I know what I said, Unnati, and now this is what I'm saying, because I was lying before, and now I'm not…' *But I am!*

'Arnold committed suicide. He jumped from my building's terrace and smashed into a thousand little pieces on the footpath.'

'You fucking bastard! You killed him!'

'I didn't! He killed himself!'

Unnati informs Aftab of the second Arnold's excruciating birth into bondage. 'Now MmYum's won't release the second Arnold unless the first one returns to take his place.'

Aftab chuckles bitterly. 'Brilliant. From a country of over a billion people, you can only find non-human clowns to worry about.'

'Excuse me, I didn't choose this battle!'

'The first Arnold was a great opportunity, but we lost him and now it's over. What do you want to do? Pay for the second Arnold's release? And what if the one after him comes alive as well? How many clowns will you rescue? How many will you stop from committing suicide? Don't stretch this, babe. Go back to finishing your magnum opus. Go join an NGO if nothing's coming. There are thousands out there who could use your help—real people of flesh and blood: bar girls, Biharis, Muslims, Dalits… Get off the stupid clowns!'

Unnati considers the possibility that this time, despite his avowals to the contrary, Aftab might actually be lying. Whoever heard of mascot-clowns committing suicide? Lemmings and rock stars, yes. Mascot-clowns? No chance.

But if the first Arnold was still alive and out there, why hadn't he returned to the downtown Mumbai branch? Could he have lost his way? Unnati imagines the vulnerable clown stumbling about the city's nasty streets. She feels an intense wave of pity arising and then…

And then a sudden realization.

Her anxiety subsides. Unnati is overcome with a feeling of tranquility. A beatific smile invades her face. She giggles at herself. How silly, getting so worked up over an allegory. It didn't really matter whether the first Arnold was alive or dead, or whether the second Arnold obtains his freedom. The clowns' destinies were mere symbolic gestures serving a higher purpose. Allegories proceeded with their own internal logic until they ran out of juice. Unnati's meddling would only delay the inevitable. There was nothing anyone could do, least of all a struggling writer like Unnati.

Unnati turns on her laptop. She remembers she has her own unfinished allegories to bring home.

Clown Karma

The manager of MmYum's downtown Mumbai branch had given Unnati a twenty-four-hour deadline to locate the first Arnold. The manager waits two extra days for Unnati to show up. By the fourth day of her non-appearance it was clear that she had failed and that the first Arnold would never, ever return.

The second Arnold seems to pick up on the bad news. He becomes subdued and silent; so still, in fact, that the staff at MmYum's wonders if he has died. He stops thrashing about on his bench or straining against the screws in his limbs. He no longer growls when someone approaches him.

One night after closing, the manager makes his way to the clown, past the fortress of tables and chairs surrounding the bench. He studies the second Arnold for a couple of minutes. Not a twitch. Without warning, the manager yanks the cloth covering Arnold's mouth. The clown was now free to speak, to scream, to let loose some expletives. Not a sound.

'Arnold, I have to tell you something,' the manager says. 'You have to remain here forever. The first Arnold hasn't come back to take your place. We can't let you go. Not now. Not ever.'

A single shudder passes through Arnold's body, rattling the bench for three seconds. And then nothing. The clown remains mute and unmoving; the eerie smile on his plasto-plastic face remaining wider than ever.

The next morning, seven days after the second Arnold had gained sentience, the alfresco section of the downtown Mumbai branch is once again thrown open to public. Tables and chairs are set up around Arnold's bench. The blue plastic sheets are draped over the roof as reinforcement against the rains.

MmYum's employees watch anxiously as customers begin filing in.

Clown-deprived children make a beeline for the second Arnold. They tweak his nose and poke his groin and heap abuse on the clown. Two guys from Takeaway remain at hand in case Arnold acts up. No such thing happens.

In a couple of days, everyone forgets that the second Arnold had ever been alive.

Everyone except the children.

MmYum's kiddy customers seem to intuitively know that their beloved clown in their most favourite restaurant is awake and watching them. They begin to crowd around Arnold like ants around sugar. 'I know you can see me,' they whisper in his ears. They gaze into his wide-open eyes and pull the most hilarious funny faces. Desperate to provoke a reaction from Arnold, the children creep up from behind his bench and spring into his lap. The kids' boos and yeaaahs startle the adult diners and MmYum's staff. However, no matter what the kids do, the intended beneficiary of their attention-seeking antics remains unresponsive.

Doesn't Arnold hear and see any of this? Of course he does. Often, late at night, upon recalling the amusing expressions of some adorable child, the clown sniggers to himself. His creepy chortles disturb the stillness of the shadowy alfresco section, making the night watchman's skin crawl.

Arnold longs to pull a prank of his own. He imagines the panic that would ensue if he were to suddenly respond to the children's incessant pestering. Would the kids scream and run away? Would they poop their pants? Would they die of shock? What difference would it make, anyway? Even if the whole world were to learn of the second Arnold's sentience, the clown would still have to remain on his bench, nailed down and trapped like a butterfly specimen.

During school days and at exam time, the downtown Mumbai branch saw few underaged patrons. Finding the clown's bench free of kids, adult clients would muster up the audacity to approach Arnold. For Arnold, this was hands down the worst aspect of his job. In the clown's proximity, smartly dressed grown-ups regressed in seconds to their juvenile past selves. Gangs of squealing, overweight housewives took turns to pose for photos in Arnold's lap. Packs of executives from neighbouring offices draped their paws around Arnold's shoulders and groped the clown's void crotch to feel good about their own ample-in-comparison groins. Arnold cringed and shivered for hours after.

On one such child-free afternoon at the restaurant, two T-shirt-and-jeans-clad men saunter over to the clown's bench. They sidle up to him on either side. The man on the right touches Arnold's knee. The other man runs his hand over Arnold's left arm, starting with the clown's shoulder. Arnold steels himself for a revolting session of heavy petting.

And then…

'Shit!' the arm-stroker mutters. 'The left hand's screwed to the bench.'

The knee-patter checks Arnold's other hand. 'This one too.'

The two men try to push Arnold. 'The legs too, they've been screwed to the floor.'

They scope out the rest of Arnold's body for more points of fastening.

'Good thing we came to check,' the knee-patter says.

'We better come prepared with pliers,' the arm-stroker says.

The two sit on the bench for some more time, pretending to be mates on a harmless junk-meal outing.

'He's creepy, this clown,' observes the arm-stroker.

'Who cares, comrade, as long as he burns well.'

They both laugh and get up to go. 'See you soon, Arnold MmYum!'

Burns well? The clown's head turns woozy with terror and excitement and impatience and unadulterated existential dread. When? Bloody hell, when? By the time it occurs to Arnold to demand a time frame from his would-be arsonists, the two men have already slunk away.

That evening, Arnold breaks his silence for the first time in weeks. He calls out to a woman from the cleaning staff, a fresher who began duty just a week and a half ago. The woman had no idea that the mascot-clown she'd been dusting and spray-cleaning all these days was in fact alive. When she realizes that it is Arnold MmYum psst-pssting to her from his bench, the woman faints. The branch manager is mortified at the ensuing scene. The unconscious woman is hauled through the crowded restaurant to the back office, past the saucer-eyed stares of alarmed children.

'The clown!' the woman whispers to the manager on coming to. 'He... he spoke to me!'

Frustrated by delayed supplies, staff perpetually late or absent, a fascist head office, and ever-increasing crowds on train rides to and from work, this was the last thing the manager needed to hear. He orders the alfresco section closed… yet again.

The two watchmen usher dozens of protesting diners into the main restaurant. The manager glowers at the motionless clown from a distance. From among 121 MmYum's branches throughout the country, did these fucking clowns have to come alive only at the downtown Mumbai branch? The manager had already screwed down the second Arnold's hands and legs; it is now time, he realizes, to pinion the clown's soul.

'What the fuck, haanh?' the manager yells as he approaches Arnold's bench. The lights of the alfresco section had been turned off and the music turned up loud so that no one could hear or witness the unthinkable cruelty of the manager's words.

'I'm really sorry,' the clown says. 'Is that woman okay? I didn't mean to scare…'

The manager slaps Arnold on his mouth.

The clown starts to whimper.

'Fuck you, you're sorry. Fucking clown. Don't pull this shit again, you hear me…'

'But I…'

'Shut the fuck up! I talk, you listen!'

The manager stands before Arnold, forcing the latter to look up like a child.

'I don't know why you're even alive. You're not supposed to be alive. Go back to whatever clown paradise you've come from. We run a business here, and you're just a prop, a fucking mascot…'

'There were two men today!' Arnold cries out. 'They said they would burn me!'

'I hope they do! I hope they roast you like chicken tikka and throw you in some gutter. You're a mistake, Arnold MmYum, a freak of the natural laws of consciousness. You and the clown before you…'

The manager should have stopped right there. Any mention of the first clown was enough to take the wind out of the second one. Nothing depressed the second Arnold more than the memory of having been let down and forsaken by one of his kind.

'We don't care if you die, we don't care if the roof comes crashing down and flattens you like a roti. You are inconsequential. There are dozens of mascot-clowns like you being manufactured even as we speak. In fact…' and here the manager meant to fib for effect, unaware that his imaginative lie would come true in a couple of months, 'headquarters at Cleveland is thinking of replacing the MmYum's mascot. No more clowns, you understand? Soon you won't even be needed here. We'll parcel you to some village in Uttar Pradesh where you'll be dressed up in rags and planted in the middle of a field to scare away the birds…'

Arnold does not speak again after that evening. Devastated and disillusioned by the branch manager's vicious barrage, he ceases to chuckle to himself in the nights.

Sensing that the vibrancy has vanished from Arnold, even the children muffle their exuberance around the mascot-clown.

The manager's brutal words continue to ricochet inside Arnold's hollow head. *Fucking mascot. Prop. Inconsequential. Soon you won't even be needed here. Go back to whatever clown paradise you've come from.*

Eight slow-moving, sorrowful days later, Arnold's two would-be arsonists return to MmYum's with their band of 'comrades'. By then, the disheartened and crushed mascot-clown had become resigned to the idea of his fiery and gruesome annihilation.

Paper Tigers

On the morning of the day of his proposed incineration, a canvas sheet is draped over Arnold on account of an impromptu paint job being carried out on the wall behind his bench. Unable to see, the clown's hearing becomes keener than usual.

He senses chaos all morning. By afternoon, Arnold can feel definite trouble in the air. Somewhere in the distance, someone starts speaking into a loudspeaker. The continuous wails of police sirens are punctuated by the hoots and screeches of a mob. Arnold begins to hear men and women barking slogans.

The sloganeering seems to get closer.

'AMERCA, hai-hai! SPMA, hai-hai!'

'No port, no pact, SPMA go back!'

'Everyone says the same, our PM is lame-lame-lame!'

'Jay Rai, hai-hai! Wendy Fernando, hai-hai!'

Soon there is pandemonium all around Arnold. He can hear children and adults screaming, the crash of furniture, the strident orders of men and the shrill cries of women. A loud clatter goes off behind Arnold. The painter's ladder? Metal strikes metal somewhere in the foreground. Everything goes quiet all of a sudden—the alfresco section, the street outside; silence everywhere. In that short-lived interval of stillness, Arnold hears the faraway growl of thousands of people.

The next moment the canvas is pulled away and Arnold is blinded by the glare.

The mascot-clown finds himself surrounded by a group of men and women. They are armed with stones and pipes. Two men set to work trying to dislodge the screw from Arnold's left hand.

The street outside is ablaze under the afternoon sun. The rest of the alfresco section is devoid of customers. Tables and chairs have been knocked over. Trays of food lie strewn all over the slate floor; sandwiches and onion rings dot the tiles amid growing lakes of sodas and shakes.

A throng of terrified-looking children and adults peer out from behind the full-length glass windows of MmYum's main restaurant. Among them are staff members in their orange T-shirts and green caps and the manager in his striped short-sleeve shirt. *Speak up, Arnold! Move! Do something!* The manager and his staff are yelling themselves hoarse, urging the chain store's mascot-clown to reveal his sentience and to save himself from the rioters who had taken over the alfresco section.

On the other side of the soundproof glass, Arnold misinterprets their gesticulations as signs of displeasure. The clown resolves not to move no matter what happens, if that's what his colleagues (in a manner of speaking) were so desperately urging him to do.

The rioters pry Arnold loose limb by limb. The screw in his ankles is over seven inches long. After much unsuccessful loosening, it is yanked out like a rotten tooth by a man whom Arnold recognizes immediately. One of his would-be arsonists! The end was near!

'Hirst Inc., hai-hai! AMERCA, hai-hai!'

'SPMA, go home, go home! SPMA...'

'Jay Rai, hai-hai! Wendy Fernando, hai-hai!'

Arnold has no idea what these slogans mean, or why the people chanting them look so furious. He glances at the restaurant one last time. The people inside have shrunk back from the glass windows after being menaced by a brick-wielding young woman.

It takes four men, two under each outstretched plasto-plastic arm, to lift the mascot-clown's unwieldy body. Arnold continues to maintain his seated posture of bent knees and crossed ankles. The rioters nearly slip on the trays of Yuma and YumYuma Meals which they'd flung to the floor. Like a child held aloft (or like a sozzled sot), Arnold swings between the four men as they dodge sandwiches and puddles of soft drinks.

Once they've managed to carry the second Arnold out of MmYum's and into the street, the clown's abductors are rejuvenated by the success of their mission. They resume their sloganeering with renewed vigour:

'No port! No pact! SPMA go back!'

'MmYum's, hai-hai! Neo-imperialism, hai-hai!'

'Jay Rai, hai-hai! AMERCA, hai-hai!'

Arnold was being hauled off to Azad Maidan, the Freedom Ground, where a massive protest rally against the Amboi Port was under way. The show-stopper of the rally was going to be the dropping of Arnold MmYum into a burning barrel.

It was anyone's guess how the cremation of a mascot-clown would address the dispossession of rural folks hundreds of kilometres away. MmYum's had nothing to do with the proposed Amboi Port project, or with SPMA, the port's financial backers, or with Hirst Inc., the port's technical advisors, or with AMERCA, the firm that would own and run the port under the chiefdom of Jay Rai and Wendy Fernando. It was true that the Amboi project was a true-blue neo-liberal swindle that would oust thousands of farmers, fisherfolk, ranchers and forest dwellers from their centuries-old homes and villages. But good ol' junk-peddling, cholesterol-disseminating MmYum's had absolutely no stake in this ecologically devastating and life-ruining crime of an undertaking. Evidently, then, the decision to incinerate Arnold the clown was based on little more than the random whim of a handful of demented do-gooders.

'Where will all the homeless go? State government, go slow, go slow!'

'Hirst Inc., hai-hai!'

'Wendy and Jay, hai-hai!'

'AMERCA, hai-hai!'

'SPMA, hai-hai!'

It all becomes too much for Arnold: the hundreds of agitators, the riot police, the traffic jam, the wails of sirens and blaring of car horns. Somewhere between Gaffur Watch Company and Capital Cinema, the clown passes out. His six-week-old consciousness was still fragile. While his senses were blown by the excess of sensory stimuli, the clown's outward demeanour remains unchanged. He stays stiffly suspended between the four men, with arms outstretched, head tilted forward and knees bent. As their procession inches towards the maidan, Arnold's abductors remain blithely unaware of the waxing and waning of their hostage's state of consciousness. Along the way, Arnold's group encounters belligerent stares from the largely rural crowd of protestors who were sickened by how these city-based activists, by parading a stupid clown, seemed to be belittling the seriousness of their crisis.

When Arnold comes to several minutes later, he finds the scene around him has turned even more tumultuous. He was being carried through the gates of the maidan. The number of people had multiplied manifold. A woman's voice was blasting through scores of loudspeakers. The air pulsated with the frenzied cheering of thousands of demonstrators gathered in the ground. There was drum-beating and whistle-blowing and waving banners and people in Manmohan masks, and the flying forms of startled birds darkened against the blazing afternoon sun…

Arnold misses his peaceful days at MmYum's. All he'd wanted

was to be freed from the screws. This chaos and the milling mobs were giving him the shakes.

The procession carrying the clown is held up at an overcrowded entrance to the backstage area.

'And why wouldn't they, friends?' the woman bellows on stage. 'Who wouldn't want to take advantage? They are being invited with open arms to pump away between our nation's parted legs. But look carefully, see who is holding our nation's legs apart. Study those pimping hands. Learn the shapes of those fingers by heart. When the next election comes around, it'll be those same paws, joined together in beseeching namastes, begging you for your votes...'

The crowd roars its approval. The woman beams. Trashing politicians always worked.

The clown blanks out.

The backstage area throbbed with the agitated presence of radicals, writers, heads of NGOs, human rights activists, as well as representatives of the APAPA, who were quite frankly outnumbered and outclassed by their sophisticated and slick-tongued urban counterparts. Among the personalities present backstage was JD, the icy-eyed bald man who once sat at the first Arnold's feet in Aftab's home. JD was legal advisor to a group demanding children's right to employment, a liberty the nation's underaged citizens were being denied under new-fangled labour laws. When Arnold was carried in, the people backstage greeted the new arrival and his abductors with understandable coldness. What a silly and ill-timed attempt at satire! The organizers of the rally would've liked to banish this freak show. However, having promised an unrestricted platform to all APAPA-sympathizing groups and individuals, provided they wrapped up their speeches in under ten minutes (and contributed one thousand rupees towards logistical expenses), the organizers were duty bound to allow Arnold's abductors the chance to air their views. While others shunned the new comers, icy-eyed JD studied the clown for some sign of sentience.

Two speakers were already lined up to go on stage. Arnold's posse gets in line as well. Over the next twenty minutes, as the group awaits their turn, the clown faints and regains consciousness several times. On each occasion that he comes to, Arnold finds himself a little closer to the stage, propped up variously against bamboo scaffolding, atop a table, and at one time, when all Arnold can see is a maroon canvas sky, he realizes he has been placed face-up on the floor.

When it is finally the turn of Arnold's group to go up on stage and address the rally, the clown is still out cold. As a result, Arnold misses the boisterous reception that he receives when his stiff, comatose form is carried onto the stage before thousands of people.

Having endured the grave—and often grating—speeches by successive speakers since early afternoon, the audience in the maidan was ready for some fun. The appearance of a mascot-clown on stage was a sign of the first-class tomfoolery to follow.

Arnold's abductors had come prepared to play to the gallery.

The clown is set down on a white plastic chair in the middle of the stage.

His abductors adorn the clown with a garland of old shoes.

They empty a household trash can into his lap.

They place a conical star-spangled cap over his green head.

And then, while four of them slip away for other preparations, three of Arnold's abductors stand to one side of the clown and stare expressionlessly at the sea of spectators.

People couldn't decide what was funnier: a despoiled

international mascot-clown with his arms stretched into the air and an ecstatic grin on his acrylic face, or his deadpan abductors gazing dumbly into space.

Precious seconds tick by. The clapping and laughter peter out. With only a few minutes to go before their ten minutes are up, one of Arnold's abductors, a bespectacled middle-aged man in a green shirt and ragged jeans, steps up to the mike. He joins his raised hands over his head:

'Greetings to you all from the Indian chapter of Paper Tigers! We've only paid for ten minutes of air time, and we've already squandered half of them, so I'll make this quick...'

As he speaks, a massive metal drum is dragged in front of the stage. One of Arnold's abductors, a woman in a tank top and black gypsy skirt, throws in a lit match. The drum turns into a vessel of towering flames. Behind the invisible screen of hot air, the man speaking on stage seems like a mirage to the crowd, wavy and insubstantial, which is just as well, because he has nothing momentous to say.

Blah, blah, blah...

'We cannot tolerate...'

Yada, yada...

'Oppose the branded blandness...'

Dot, dot, dot...

'Is a symbol of neo-liberal fascim and Western hegemony...'

Yawn, snore, zzzzzzz...

As the man drones on, two other members of Paper Tigers slide under Arnold's arms and carry him to the edge of the stage. The clown was now directly above the flaming barrel that had begun to sizzle and steam like a bakery oven.

'This is not just a clown, friends, he is the epitome of all that is rotten about a world where profit dictates everything!'

The speaker knocks the star-spangled cap off Arnold's head. He screams into the mike, 'Burn, you emblem of capitalist greed and consumerist stupidity, burn!'

The garbage had fallen off Arnold's lap. Now the cap was gone, too. The only remaining sign of the clown's dishonour was the garland of shoes around his neck.

'Come on, friends!' the speaker urges the crowd: 'Arnold! Arnold! Arnold! Arnold!'

The audience in the maidan obliges by setting up a steady chant.

'Arnold! Arnold! Arnold! Arnold!'

It was staggering, thousands of people intoning the name of a doomed mascot-clown.

'Arnold! Arnold! Arnold! Arnold!'

It was loud enough to interrupt conversations throughout the neighbourhood.

'Arnold! Arnold! Arnold! Arnold!'

Loud enough to shake up floors of heritage structures in the vicinity.

'Arnold! Arnold! Arnold! Arnold!'

Loud enough to cross the permissible sound limit for open-air gatherings.

'Arnold! Arnold! Arnold! Arnold!'

Loud enough for the superintendent of riot police to order the activation of water cannons.

'Arnold! Arnold! Arnold! Arnold!'

And loud enough to jolt the ill-fated mascot-clown back to his senses.

'Arnold! Arnold! Arnold! Arnold!'

It is a scene the second Arnold would not forget until his 'dying day' (which would be ten and a half months later, by the side of a mountain, his acrylic body being torn apart from within by the flourishing roots of a jamun tree).

There were people, people, and more people as far as the clown could see, and this teeming, restless and uproarious mass of humanity had only one word on its lips: Arnold! Arnold! Arnold!

'Don't give up, amigos!' the speaker on stage begs the crowd. 'Let's get louder! Let's shake up headquarters! All the way to Cleeeeeavelaaand!'

'Arnold!'

'Arnold!'

'Arnold!'

'Arnold!'

'Arnold!'

Suspended between the two men before the sea of spectators, Arnold becomes convinced that humans were crazy nuts. This hero's welcome for someone who was going to be burned? Such a resounding reception for someone who, in the branch manager's words, was an inconsequential fucking mascot? At every echo of his moniker, Arnold grows more impatient with this stupid farce that seemed to just stretch and stretch. If that fire raging a couple of feet away was for him, why didn't they just toss him in and be done with it.

The clown shifts his weight forward. The men holding him up experience a sudden increase in load. They frown at one another; each of them is convinced that the other is trying to lessen his burden. Arnold had no intention of killing himself. He merely wished to investigate the source of the flames. He continues to lean forward, making it difficult for the men under his outstretched arms to hold him up.

The man on the right stumbles. The man on the left fails to catch the slipping clown. Arnold keels to one side. Pushed to his knees under the weight of Arnold's bulk, the man on the right finds himself teetering on the edge of the stage, staring into the flaming barrel.

'Ooh!' The crowd lets out a collective intake of air.

Despite his best attempts to slough off the clown, the man on the right, before the horrified gaze of thousands, falls over head-first into his near-certain fiery death.

Arnold follows suit the next instant, and is swept away in a gush of water so powerful that it shreds his garland of shoes and hurls him, the man who fell before him, and the flaming barrel (now doused) towards the scattering crowd at a speed of 100 kilometres per hour.

Hard-boiled radicals gain a new-found respect for water cannons that afternoon. Thanks to the readiness of the riot police, the clumsy member of Paper Tigers is saved from being roasted to death.

It takes three concentrated jets of water less than fifteen minutes to clear the whole of Azad Maidan. Thousands of demonstrators, speakers, bystanders, hawkers, villagers, invited dignitaries and a lone clown are hosed back in a helpless and soggy ebb of heads and legs, bags and banners, shoes and spectacles…

As soon as he falls off the stage, Arnold grabs the first thing that comes to hand and doesn't let go until he comes to rest on a footpath half a kilometre away, surrounded by hundreds of other people who were soaked to the bone and laughing and giggling in spite of themselves. An anti-port protest couldn't have asked for a wetter end.

Arnold pries away a dripping dupatta from his head. He realizes that he had been clutching someone's bare foot. This foot was joined to a leg clad in grey trousers, and the trousers to the body of a man who was sitting on the footpath and staring at Arnold in utter disbelief. It was the member of Paper Tigers, the man on the right, who'd slipped and fallen ahead of Arnold.

Arnold jerks his hand off the man's foot and stands up. 'I'm sorry.'

'Are you kidding me?' The man stands up as well, barely reaching Arnold's shoulder. 'I should be saying sorry! We're all sorry for trying to burn you! If we'd known you were alive... Why didn't you give us some sign, some clue?'

All around them, were drenched men and women struggling to get to their feet. People were clearing their bodies of leaves, wet mud and other people's belongings that had washed up on them like debris. As office-goers rushed to catch their evening trains, they wondered if all these soaked folks had fallen from the sky.

Arnold starts to walk away. He didn't know where to go. Too much had happened too soon.

'Wait!' the man begins running after the clown. 'Wait, where are you going?'

Considering the fellow and his cohorts had damn-near burned him, Arnold didn't think he was obliged to respond.

'Hey, listen, clown guy, hold up!'

Arnold stops. 'What now? You want to burn me again?'

The crowd had begun dispersing.

'I don't understand,' the clown shakes his head and looks around, as if the answer lay somewhere in the air. 'I was just sitting on my bench until you people came along, wanting to burn me. What wrong did I do to any of you?'

Wow, what a mind job! The man wishes his comrades were around. This was too fantastic to be experienced alone.

'I know I have a lot to explain. Can we sit first?'

Arnold was in no mood to obey.

'Please, my friend,' the man insists. 'I'm still shaken from that fall. I almost died too, you know.'

They were at the Hutatma Chowk intersection, where traffic went around garden islands dedicated to statues of India's post-colonial luminaries. Within a stone's throw from one another were Gandhi, Nehru, Bose, Tagore, Indira and Rajiv, captured in bronze, steel and cast iron, portrayed as the patriots, visionaries, brave-hearts and magnificent orators that they (sometimes) were. The man leads the reluctant clown to a patch of green across the road. They dodge traffic, jump a fence and sit down under the shadow of a cast-iron Ambedkar statue.

Several cracks had formed on the clown's acrylic body, along his arms and legs; there was a deep dent on his right hip, where the jet of water probably hit.

'My school used to be just around the corner,' the man says, pointing to the left, 'my friends and I would come and sit here during lunch breaks. They didn't have these fences back then. You could sit and nap anywhere you liked.'

Arnold wonders whether he was being missed at MmYum's. Or was he being blamed for his own abduction?

'You want to know why we tried to burn you? Believe me, it wasn't personal. To us, you were no more alive than these statues around us. In fact, after meeting you, I'm not so sure if these statues are as lifeless as they profess to be…'

Arnold looks up at the Ambedkar figure. It was a tantalizing notion.

'Anyway, I digress. We wanted to burn you because we can't burn the people we really want to burn. It's called symbolism. No offence, but you are a symbol of so many things that we loathe. By attacking you, we wanted to voice our figurative protest against corporate greed and governmental collusion. Is any of this making sense to you, Arnold?'

Of course it made sense to Arnold. He wasn't stupid. 'I am a symbol. You hate me and want to burn me.'

'No, no, Arnold, we don't hate *you*! We hate what you stand for, what you sym-bo-lize...'

The clown remains silent. It sounded like splitting hairs to him.

The man pulls out a checkered handkerchief and begins to rub his damp hair.

Arnold plucks blades of grass from the ground.

'How...'

The man stops mid-rub and waits for the clown to continue.

'How do I stop symbolizing what you hate? How do I become me, just me, not something that people like you want to attack and burn?'

The man becomes lost in thought. He had never encountered such a pitiful plea for acceptance. 'Oh, I... I can't say, Arnold. I've never thought of it from your point of view. It's not every day that plastic effigies come alive and start talking.'

But they do, Arnold argues quietly. He tosses away the handful of grass. He remembers the first Arnold and wonders if his predecessor was also being targeted for what he symbolized. Had anyone ever tried to attack or destroy the first Arnold? Was it possible that he hadn't been as lucky as the second Arnold? The first Arnold's death, even as an idea, was unbearable to the second one. Despite resenting his predecessor, the second Arnold found himself hoping for his well-being. No matter what they stand for or symbolize, no one, not even clowns, deserve to be burned.

After the washout of a rally, most city protestors had started to go their own ways, leaving hundreds of rural folks stranded on the footpaths outside Azad Maidan. In the water-cannon-induced bedlam, villagers got separated from fellow villagers and family members lost sight of each other. Worsening the situation was the city's remorseless rush-hour traffic—both four-wheeled and two-legged. Disoriented villagers in their ragged and rustic finery rushed about outside swish shops and restaurants, yelling out the names of brothers, sisters, spouses and friends.

From their island of refuge, under the aegis of the Ambedkar statue, Arnold and his failed arsonist watch the disorder with detachment.

'As usual,' the man snorts, 'it's the poor who are left holding the cheque.'

A posse of lathi-wielding policemen descend on the villagers, beating them back from the edge of the road.

'The bastards!'

And then there he was, surfacing from the crowd in his striped short-sleeved shirt, accompanied by a policeman, the person Arnold had hoped never to see again, his bête noire and tormentor par excellence—the manager of MmYum's downtown Mumbai branch. He stands on the footpath across the road and scans the landscape like a hawk.

'I have to go!' Arnold yelps. He scrambles to his feet.

'What? Where are you going?' His failed arsonist looks about in confusion.

The clown jumps over the fence and starts fleeing in the opposite direction.

The member of Paper Tigers jumps up and starts running after the clown. 'Arnold, wait! Where are you going!'

A policeman blows his whistle.

Someone yells, 'Catch that clown!'

There is no more clown. There is just a blur of green, red

and orange whizzing through the city's crowded streets at an impossible speed.

Arnold runs and runs, sidestepping pedestrians, weaving through traffic and bounding over barricades. The wind rushes into him through the holes in his hands and ankles. He feels like a hasty parcel of breeze. Arnold passes by residential buildings, school campuses and gigantic shopping malls. He is appalled by the squalor, the overall shabbiness that greets him at every turn.

He runs past several MmYum's outlets and sees several clowns like himself seated on benches outside their respective restaurants. Their immobility breaks his heart. How defenceless these clowns were; how vulnerable each of them was to the next band of goons out to make a figurative protest against capitalist greed.

Arnold is energized by his panic. His pursuer is slowed down by the absence of footwear and his smoker's lungs. The distance between them grows.

At some point, the member of Paper Tigers shouts, 'Stop, Arnold, we're far enough! There's no one following us!'

The clown seizes the chance to make a clean break. He runs faster and faster till he has left his failed arsonist and the man's hateful symbolic politics far, far behind.

End of the Road: Ferozpur Janata Express

Night had fallen. Traffic had thinned. The clown had been running for hours. He crossed the city's limits and was now in the distant suburbs, where open gutters flow past low-income housing complexes and tin-shed tenements.

Through the open windows of modest homes, Arnold spies on families eating in front of television sets, women busy in kitchens, children sprawled on floors with their books while men relaxed on beds with the dailies. Jogging past the tableaux of domestic cosiness was the scarred mascot-clown, a breakaway twig adrift in the wind.

The elation of escape had soured. Arnold was now filled with dread. When he craved for liberation during his days at MmYum's, this isn't what he had in mind—this boundless, dizzying freedom. Arnold wanted to stop running; but when? And for what?

As the night progresses, the sight of a clown dashing through the deserted streets begins to attract the wrong kind of attention. Dogs bark. Building watchmen perk up. Members of street gangs alert each other on cell phones.

The clown realizes it was a mistake to abandon the company of his failed arsonist. That man's hatred for MmYum's was almost equal to Arnold's. Besides, he'd been magnanimous enough to apologize for attempting to burn the mascot.

Arnold feels sick with regret for having ditched a potential friend and guardian. Halfway across an elevated walkway, high above a high-speed expressway, Arnold comes to a halt. He had to go back. He had to find the man who tried to burn him. The clown is gripped with the impossible hope of finding his co-runner at the exact spot where he outran him. Failing that, the clown feels foolishly certain that he will find the man sleeping under one of those statues at the Hutatma Chowk intersection.

Arnold turns around and starts retracing his steps. Crazed by desperation, he doesn't ponder over the futility of his quest. Of course he doesn't remember where he came from. Of course he begins to take all the wrong turns. The further he runs, the further the clown gets entangled in the city's labyrinthine layout. Nothing seems familiar to him—the streets, the intersections, the buildings, the bridges. It is as if he was running back through a different city. He begins whining in panic. He was tired, terrified and lost. The troublemakers steer clear of the clown as he scrambles past them. As per the strict codes of immorality binding the city's crooks, the crazies were not to be touched.

Arnold runs into an unguarded railway crossing. A packed stationary train lay in his path. He rushes up to the train and stops outside the doorway of a crowded compartment. With their deadpan, seen-it-all eyes, the throng of passengers absorb the clown's improbable presence here, outside their coach, on these darkened railway tracks in the middle of nowhere.

Impatient to resume his return run, Arnold peers to the left and right. The train stretches equally on either side. He looks back at the random street from where he came. Turning around would be pointless. One street was as good as the next for the lost clown.

A passenger in the train pushes his way to the front of the doorway. He leans out of the train and spits a voluminous arch of red liquid, missing the clown by inches.

'Sorry, didn't see you in the dark!' the man calls out to Arnold. He too begins peering to the left and right. Scores of other people down the length of the train had stuck out their heads. The delay was unprecedented.

Arnold waits.

'What are you waiting for?' the spitter asks the clown.

The clown looks up.

The man flicks his eyebrows questioningly.

'I need to go to the other side.'

I need to get back where I started.

'You should go through the train!' The spitter stretches down his arm. 'Come on, come in and jump out from the opposite door. Sometimes these trains don't move for hours!'

Arnold would forever marvel at this twist of fate that got him aboard the Ferozpur Janata Express.

He grabs the spitter's hand and hauls himself up into the compartment.

'Wow, you're light!' The man pats the mascot on the arm. 'Go on, hurry!'

Arnold is dumbstruck. Spread out before him like a thicket of humanity are more than thirty people, packed on the floor of the compartment between the two doorways. Beggars, mostly, and hobos, drug addicts and gypsy families—people who sit or sleep anywhere and have long ceased to care about the contamination of their bodies. Huddled on the left, outside the stinking toilets, is a squad of eunuchs preparing themselves for yet another night of beggary and buggery.

Arnold begins wading through the crowd. 'Excuse me… I'm sorry… Need to get to the other side… Sorry… Side please… Excuse me…'

They hardly move, these people. They look up at the clown with their yellow vacant eyes and don't seem to mind if he pushes them with his legs or walks over their mucky feet.

A eunuch grabs the mascot's plasto-plastic foot as he passes by. 'Oye hero, spare some change here!'

Arnold doesn't make it.

The train shudders to life when the clown is just about halfway through. He looks back in panic, at the passenger who'd suggested this antic.

The man flashes a red paan-stained grin and shouts from the doorway, 'Don't worry, boss, get off at the next stop!'

No one informs the poor clown that the next stop on the Ferozpur Janata was two hours and sixty-five kilometres away.

Within minutes, the train assumes a speed that substantiates its 'Express' tag.

Arnold begins to get in the way of passengers needing to use the loo. The people on the floor leave little space for shuffling around. Unable to go past, a fat saree-clad woman carrying an overweight toddler berates the clown in a loud voice, 'O brother, why don't you stop being a nuisance and get a seat!'

Aware of his acrylic vulnerability, Arnold mumbles, 'Good idea!' and ducks out of the behemoth's path.

The first booth offers no seating space. The second booth is likewise chock-full. Scruffy, malnourished men and women in ill-fitting clothes eye the mascot with disinterest as he passes by their seats. Outside the barred windows the landscape is eerily dark. Never mind the train's dinginess and the jam; Arnold was glad to be in here and not out there.

In the fourth booth, without being asked, a young man shifts away from the corner edge of his berth. Arnold swoops in on the sliver of seating space and acknowledges the man's kindness with a nod.

Most passengers are dozing. The waking ones merely stare: straight ahead, at each other, or outside the windows, where there is nothing to see. Two booths away, somebody switches on his cell phone's radio to speaker mode. The melancholy melody of an old film song strains to be heard over the roar of the warm night wind whipping in through the windows. The train's velocity was astonishing; Arnold felt silly for having run through the city for hours like a maniac; all he ought to have done is hop on to one of these speeding giants. As the train hurtles towards its unknown destination, Arnold knows that there is no going back. He was too far gone from where he'd begun.

'Chai bolo, chai...'

'Paani, water pouch! Paani, water pouch...'

'Garma garam idli! Idli bolo...'

'Peroo! Peroo ley lo, peroo...'

'Goa, paan masala, cigarette, lighter...'

'Sing, chana, time pass! Sing, chana, time pass...'

Half an hour into the journey, the gangways of the Ferozpur Janata Express are transformed into a boisterous thoroughfare for small-time entrepreneurs and food vendors from the hinterland. Dirt-poor businessmen and businesswomen attempted to arouse the appetites and curiosity of dirt-poor passengers. Despite the unhygienic food, the questionable purity of the beverages and the evident shoddiness of the China-made gewgaws, there were enough transactions happening to revive every starving belly and to keep aloft every sinking household.

The passenger seated beside Arnold notices that the clown hadn't purchased any of the meagre eatables on sale—not even the spiced peanuts, a handful of which cost a few rupees, something that even the most down-and-out traveller indulged in. Overcoming his shyness, Arnold's co-passenger tilts his cone of spiced peanuts towards the clown. The clown shakes his head. The man waggles the cone and goads Arnold with winks and nods. *Go on, dig in, take some.* The clown pats his hollow belly to indicate he is full-up. The man shrugs his shoulders and empties the flute of peanuts into his mouth.

Arnold watches the gobbling faces all around him in the compartment. He no longer envied those who ate. (It was a contentment stemming from resignation. One night, overcome by hunger, the clown had begged the watchman at MmYum's to feed him something, anything, because otherwise he was sure his insides would cave in. The watchman had brought a plate of egg bhurji from a neighbourhood stall servicing night-shift workers. He had deposited a few spoonfuls of the egg scramble into the clown's plastic mouth. When the clown tried to swallow, the chewed mush squelched out from the sides of his lips. It was one of the most despairing moments for Arnold—the realization that there is to be no respite from his ravenous hunger.)

The floor of the compartment becomes littered with peanut shells, fruit peels and balls of trash. After the hawkers move on to other coaches, the parasites arrive: the clapping eunuchs, the blind singers, the women with naked children, and the able-bodied drug addicts who make a show of industriousness by sweeping the compartment's floor with their own grubby garments.

Like the hawkers before them, the moochers and panhandlers are especially persistent with Arnold. They cannot believe that the clown can't spare some change. They mock his cheapness. 'All these pauper foreigners coming to our country,' a beggar woman sneers. A peeved eunuch jerks his crotch at the mascot. Like millions of others throughout the country, Arnold quickly learns that the best way to deflect these pesky scroungers was to look right through them.

It is the last half-hour before the train's first stop. Having nothing left to spare for the purveyors of junk or for the seekers of charity, the passengers in the compartment are left alone at last. A slumberous peace settles. No one speaks. No one plays music. It is the clown's first moment of calm since his abduction from MmYum's that afternoon. Scrunched up on the edge of the berth, Arnold becomes aware of the subtle delights of freedom. Freedom from the screws pinning his limbs down, freedom from a mascot's stultifying existence, and then this afternoon—

freedom from becoming a symbol of someone else's demented radical beliefs.

The clown looks down at the holes in his palms and ankles. He strokes his dented hip. He is grateful for these marks of the world's brutality. They would forever remind him—not that he would ever forget—that beneath the benign-seeming veneer of existence was the face of a killer. It is only a matter of time before the world begins to maim and cripple each of its inhabitants. The ones who lasted longest weren't necessarily blessed, they just ran the fastest. And that is what the clown intended to do: He would keep moving. Train to train. Place to place. Day and night, month upon month. Never mind where. He would undo the injustice of his bound birth by allowing himself a free run in this world.

Lulled by vivid and pleasurable fantasies of his nomadic future, the clown fails to notice the appearance of the blazer-clad and ticket-punching official whose job it was to evict all those freeloaders like Arnold who thought the Indian Railways was their fucking father's property.

Suck My Ticket Checker

'What is ticket?'

The ticket checker had never felt so offended. He was used to reprobates feigning surprise at their own ticketlessness. He was used to passengers rummaging through their pockets and purses in search of that non-existent ticket stub. In his fifteen years of employment with the Indian Railways, the TC had encountered threats and pleas to be let off, as well as fantastic excuses for non-possession of valid proof of travel. But until now, no passenger had had the audacity to question the very framework of modern mass transit. 'Excuse me? What did you say?'

Arnold repeats his query in all earnestness, 'What is ticket?'

The TC throws an incredulous look at the rifle-wielding CRPF jawan escorting him. He glances at the passengers sitting in Arnold's booth. He asks the clown, 'Did you just ask, what is ticket?'

The clown looks around. He is confused by the astonished expressions of his fellow passengers. He nods at the TC.

'Since you don't know what is ticket, I assume you don't have one?' the TC asks.

The clown nods again.

'Thought as much. Can you stand up, please?'

The clown gets to his feet. The TC has to look up to address Arnold. 'Do you know what is jail?'

Arnold shakes his head.

The TC smiles with mock benevolence. 'Don't worry, you'll know soon.' He turns to the jawan. 'Take this chap into custody.'

Arnold is staggered by the sudden turn of events. One moment he was contemplating his future on the edge of the berth; the next moment he is among a horde of drunks and crooks being herded along by the armed jawan. They were being led to the front of the train to the control room where, depending on their ability to pay the fine for ticketless travel, they would either be let off with warnings or sent to jail.

Arnold's cool act earns him the admiration of his fellow felons. As their entourage shuffles through the gangways of successive compartments, they sidle up to Arnold to befriend the genius mind among them.

'You're really smart for a clown!'

'You must be really experienced. You didn't even break into a sweat.'

'What is ticket. Haha, too good, yaar! I'll use it next time.'

Arnold keeps quiet and smiles at them all. By now he knew what a ticket was. It was the stub of crumpled paper that passengers offered to the TC when he walked into compartments and clicked his puncher. By now Arnold also knew how to behave when you didn't have one. Always express horror, always rifle through your pockets, and never, ever ask, *What is ticket.*

As they proceed through the train, the TC manages to nab several more offenders. He couldn't get Arnold out of his mind. The cheek of the fucker! He keeps looking back to ensure that Arnold hasn't escaped from the ticketless pack. He catches the jawan's eyes and motions him to keep a special watch on the clown.

The Ferozpur Janata Express approaches Vaitarna, its first stop. Half the train's passengers stand up in preparation. The jawan finds it increasingly difficult to shepherd the ticketless bunch. Their numbers begin to dwindle. Thirteen become ten. In the blink of an eye, three more crooks melt into the crowd.

There is an uproar when the train pulls into Vaitarna. The remaining seven felons, including Arnold, try to break free in the ensuing melee.

Everyone gets away. Everyone but the clown. The TC and the jawan hold on to their prize catch at the cost of the other crooks.

The TC locks his arm with Arnold's. The jawan snaps a handcuff around Arnold's left wrist.

'Now I'll show you what is ticket,' the TC announces. Stung that the others had managed to escape, the TC decides to unleash the Indian Railways' vindictive wrath upon the clown.

Arnold squirms in their ferocious grip.

'Let's get this one to the control room first,' the TC orders the jawan. 'We'll nab the others on our second round.'

They begin hauling Arnold through the remaining compartments. It was almost midnight. Passengers in the second-class compartments were settling down to a long and uncomfortable night of travel. They are startled out of their pre-sleep daze by the sight of a clown being dragged away like a dangerous criminal.

Arnold begins whimpering. 'Please, let me go, I know what is ticket, please, please let me go...'

The TC addresses the jawan over Arnold's shoulder. 'See, Guppa? Twenty minutes ago he didn't know what was ticket. Now he knows. Once we reach the control room he will start to remember the names of all his fathers.'

It takes all of Arnold's self-control to not ask, *What is father*.

There were three compartments to go before the control room: the AC second class, the AC chair car, and the most expensive of all, the AC coupés. Arnold is admonished into silence. The passengers in these compartments were affluent businessmen, members of well-known families and executives of multinationals. These latter-day royals paid hundreds of rupees extra to ensure that nothing and no one intruded upon their cocoons of silence and privacy.

Arnold lets out a gasp on being led through the AC second class. The icy air slips in through the holes in his limbs. He hates it. It feels like hundreds of frigid insects crawling around his innards. He yearns to return to the humid heat of the crowded general compartments.

The lights in the air-conditioned compartments had been dimmed. Several of the well-dressed passengers had switched on their individual reading lights. People were browsing through tablets, listening to music on their headphones, or typing away at laptops. A well-groomed face occasionally looked up deep in thought. Despite the late hour, minds in these seats were still in overdrive.

The few passengers who happen to look up recognize Arnold instantly. MmYum's was an important part of their leisure hours. It's where they took their children on weekends for expensive fast-food meals. It's where they grabbed quick bites during their hectic workdays. These passengers had taken photographs with Arnold MmYum in Paris, Houston, Tokyo, and now here he was, an international mascot-clown turned into a two-bit ragged railway delinquent. For the few passengers who happen to look up, eating at MmYum's would never be the same.

Arnold begins to drag his feet. The TC and the jawan lift him off the ground and sweep him through the chair-car section as fast as they can.

The gangway outside the AC coupés is cold and empty. At the end of the gangway is the frosted glass door that leads to the control room.

The TC opens the door with his key. The jawan unlocks the handcuff and pushes Arnold into the control room. He means to go in as well. The TC stops him. 'Let me deal with him alone. You stand here I'll call you if I need help. Let me show him what is ticket, and what is ticket checker.'

The jawan gives a crisp salute and shudders at what lies ahead for the clown.

Arnold lay on the floor, done in by fear and the bizarreness of the circumstance. The TC slides the door shut behind him. The control room was brightened by a single tube light. It was strewn with the usual railway paraphernalia: log books, signal lights, a first-aid kit and a pile of mysterious gunny bags.

The TC takes off his blazer and drapes it over a stool.

Arnold can't think of anything to say. He hopes this is the last development of his overly eventful day.

'Now you know what is ticket?' the TC asks.

Yes, yes, Arnold nods for the umpteenth time, *I know what is ticket, I know what is ticket.*

The TC unzips his trousers and fishes out his penis from the folds of his baggy underwear. He waves the tiny appendage over Arnold. 'And now I'll show you what is ticket checker.' He grabs Arnold by his acrylic chin and forces him to his knees. 'This is ticket checker. Come on, open your mouth for the ticket checker.'

Arnold looks at the man's penis. The implications of the TC's words were lost on the clown. Arnold had no sexuality capable of being degraded, and whatever offence was intended to his psyche falls way short of its mark.

'Come on! Suck!' The TC kicks Arnold between his legs. 'Suck, you fucker!'

Arnold wonders if the kick was meant to have any effect. He feels nothing.

The TC begins punching Arnold's green head. He slaps the clown's shoulders and kicks him around the control room.

Now the pain makes itself felt. Arnold, however, is beyond caring. He decides to jump off the train at the first chance he gets.

'Oh God!' the TC screams. 'Oh ma! Oh hell!' He'd forgotten to tuck away his penis, and now his trouser's zipper had bitten down on his flesh with the ferocity of a scorpion. 'See, you fucker, see what you made me do!' The TC kicks Arnold a couple of times more, worsening his own pain in the process.

The TC sits down on the blazer-draped stool. He begins

fussing over his trapped penis. Arnold sits up against a wall and waits for the performance to end.

'Ah, awoo, ah, aa, phooo, phooo, haaa, ahhh... Ahhh, my God, thank you, oh God...' Engrossed in alleviating his pain and the subsequent relief, the TC fails to heed Guppa's urgent knocks.

A kick to the door from the other side knocks the TC off his stool.

The jawan's anxious voice calls out again, 'Saab, open please, it's very important!'

The TC adjusts his attire. He slips on his blazer. He creeps up to the door and calls out, 'Guppa? What is it?'

There is another loud bang on the door. Guppa can be heard quarrelling with someone. 'Saab, a passenger from chair car wants to speak to you!'

'Open the door!' An insubstantial voice cries out from the other side. The door shakes from the force of the knocking. 'Open this door now!'

The TC storms over to Arnold and pulls him up to his feet. 'Stay put. Not a sound from you.'

He settles his hair and adjusts his spectacles one last time before raising the latch.

Guppa sticks his head in as soon as the door slides open a bit. His eyes dart about the room. When he spots Arnold standing in the corner, he lets out a howl of amazement.

The TC looks back at Arnold. He turns back to the jawan. 'What hoo hoo? What's wrong? Open the door, who's there?'

The TC shoves the door open fully. When he sees who is standing outside, he too wants to howl like the jawan.

'Have you booked my friend for an offence?' the passenger from the chair car asks.

The TC manages a mortified smile.

'What offence?'

'Ticket... ticketless travel...' the TC stutters.

The passenger unzips his waist pouch. He withdraws a thousand rupee note and waves it in the TC's face. 'Will this be enough to cover the fine?'

'Ye... yes, sir, it will, it will be more than sufficient...'

The passenger tucks the note into the TC's blazer pocket. 'Now is my friend free to go?'

'Ye... yes, sir...free to go...'

The jawan has to pull the frozen-to-the-spot TC aside.

The clown's rescuer leans into the control room. He stretches out a striped gloved hand. 'Come on, buddy, let's go.'

Arnold hesitates.

'It's OK, nothing to be afraid of. Come on, I got you.'

Arnold feels like he is walking into a mirror. He would forever marvel at the twist of fate that got him aboard the Ferozpur Janata Express.

Plasto-plastic palms clasp each other under the shell-shocked gazes of Guppa and the TC.

'You OK, Arnold?' Arnold asks.

'I'm fine, Arnold,' Arnold replies. 'Fine. A little shaken, but all right...'

One-hit-wonder Literature Festival

Welcome Kit

Welcome Letter

Welcome to the second edition of the One-hit-wonder Literature Festival. It gives us immense pleasure to have you among us.

You are here because you once mattered; you once showed buckets of promise. People still possess copies of your book. They waited and waited for the next one. Then they gave up and forgot about you. Maybe they thought you had died. This festival is to remind your past fans that you're still around.

And to ask you, what the f@#k happened?

We will not be serving alcohol this year.

Please take time to go through the welcome kit in detail. While we have covered your travel and stay, and have also committed to feed you through the days you will be attending the festival, there is, like there is with your creativity, an upper limit to our hospitality.

We will not be covering laundry, in-room dining, mini-bar expenses, Internet usage, phone calls, or any damage that you might accidentally wreak on the hotel room.

Please respect the sensibilities of the other guests in the hotel. Avoid loud conversations or watching late-night television while in your hotel room. It would be better, in fact, if you spent as little time as possible in the room allotted to you.

The venue for the festival is the Indira Gandhi Garden Estate, which is a brisk ten-minute walk from the hotel. The festival schedule is included in the welcome kit. It has probably been years, so we take the liberty to remind you of the protocol at such events: You are expected to be on time for your sessions.

We intend this to be a secure and respectful platform for the exploration of decaying creativity, broken literary promises and failure. Much of this might be painful for you to discuss. Remember, you are still loved for what you once did a long time ago. You wouldn't want to wipe away the enduring goodwill of the one good thing you've ever done, would you? Please exercise physical and verbal restraint at all times, no matter how condescending and patronizing things get.

In case you are suffering from health complications and haven't already informed the festival organizers, please do so immediately. This includes any medication that you are expected to take but are prone to deliberately skip, in an attempt to precipitate your self-destructive decline. We take no responsibility for any harm that you might knowingly inflict upon yourself.

We have tried our best to ensure that your book is available for sale at the festival venue. However, in most cases, we have been informed by publishers that the books chosen for this year's festival are unavailable or out of print. We strongly discourage you from autographing blank sheets of paper or books by other authors.

Each day will end with a musical performance and a buffet dinner. You may choose to skip the evening festivities in case the day has been too upsetting. (In which case, you will be responsible for covering your own meal expenses.)

The aim of this festival is not to fiddle with raw wounds. It is to jump-start your dormant creativity. We want you to go away energized and charged; convinced that there is still a point to writing, and that your writing in particular is still awaited by (admittedly fast-dwindling) legions of your loyal fans.

Please feel free to contact the organizers should you need any assistance during the festival. Thank you, once again, for gracing us with your presence. We hope you have a good time.

Sponsor's Letter

Dear Writer,

A very, very warm welcome to the One-hit-wonder Literature Festival. This year the festival has been sponsored by Second Chance Inverters Pvt. Ltd.

As a practitioner of a creative craft, you of all people know that embedded in every failure is an opportunity for success. We at Second Chance Inverters took that literally. We found opportunity in your power company's failure to provide its customers with 24×7 electricity.

Imagine you are on page ninety-eight of your work-in-progress literary masterpiece and suddenly there is a power failure. If you are a super-successful writer, you probably have a newish laptop with a still-functioning battery. But most writers are not so lucky and must stab away at old laptops with defunct batteries, or worse, they must use desktops with no power sources of their own. Under the sway of a literary outburst, you forgot to press Save, and now that the power is gone, you've lost almost eighteen pages of your red-hot literary manna. At such times, don't you wish you had a second chance?

You can now have a second chance in three models.

Second Chance Homeboy: This 12-kilowatt mean boy is compact enough for residential use. A half-foot cube, Homeboy can be tucked under any old piece of furniture with a wire connected to the mains. But don't be fooled by its diminutive dimensions. Homeboy can power up to three fans, two laptops and seven tube lights for almost three hours at a stretch. Homeboy comes with a two-year warranty. You can purchase Second Chance Homeboy in Jejune White, Nihilistic Black and Kitschy Grey.

The other two models include Second Chance Busybody for office use and Second Chance Strike-buster for industrial use.

Second Chance inverters are available in more than twelve countries around the world.

Second Chance Inverters Pvt. Ltd is a Ludhiana-based firm owned by the Singh family comprising three brothers and nine sisters. The Singh family has been patrons of the arts for generations. They have sponsored numerous art, film and literature events around India. Through their association with the One-hit-wonder Literature Festival, the Singh family hopes to instil a sense of confidence in writers who have been let down by their own low-powered talent battery packs and weighed down by the unfair expectations from their initial successes. A lot like a citizen fanning himself with a sheaf of electricity bills in the sweltering heat of a powerless home because someone in the power ministry was too inept or corrupt to do the one good job expected of him.

God bless you all. Have a 'powerful' time at the literature festival!

Signed,

The Singh Family

About the First Edition

Fourteen invitees. Over seventy-five footfalls. And eleven riveting sessions spread over three days. The first edition of the One-hit-wonder Literature Festival was a stupendous success. It was written about in all the major newspapers of India.

The *Hinduvani* wrote: 'The One-hit-wonder Literature Festival is proof that India's literary culture has finally come of age. It celebrates not only its success, but also sob stories.'

Mid-Noon tabloid reported: 'The festival atmosphere was a cross between a condolence meet and a very awkward Holi celebration. Move over, Jaipur! The One-hit-wonder lit fest is the writer's festival.'

Pehelzad Qureishi, one-hit-wonder author of *Hilda's Honeycombs*, claims to have got over a twelve-year-long writer's block after attending the festival. He is now on the verge of finishing his second book and is in talks with major publishers in India and around the world. 'The One-hit-wonder Literature Festival was the proverbial kick in the butt I needed,' says Qureishi. 'Alas, once I publish my second book, I will no longer qualify to be invited to the festival.'

Ipsita Gupta, one-hit-wonder author of the award-winning novel *Swinging on a Jamun Tree*, took a public oath at the festival that she would publish her second book within two years. 'The festival really shook me up. I thought people had forgotten about me. I am so glad I agreed to go to the festival. It was cathartic. It was therapeutic.'

The authors who were present at the first edition of the festival received ten kilos worth of coupons from the kind sponsors, BooksByTheKilo.com, a unique book-selling e-commerce site. (Also check out CDsByTheKilo.com, MagazinesByTheKilo.com and ArtByTheKilo.com.)

The One-hit-wonder Literature Festival invites sponsors for its third, fourth and fifth editions. Please contact Ms Shrichandani for further details.

Invitees to the Second Edition

Once upon a time, the authors invited to the One-hit-wonder Literature Festival needed no introduction. Several of them were a brand—or almost on the verge of becoming one—unto themselves. Today, however, the tide has turned. These shining stars of India's burgeoning literary scene have now gone over the horizon. Here is our attempt to dawn a new day of revival on the fortunes of these literary one-hit-wonders:

Hormuz Mistry, *Siddhartha*, HackCheck India, 1989

With *Siddhartha*, Hormuz Mistry ousted Hermann Hesse's original as the final say on Indian mysticism. While Hesse's *Siddhartha* was set in the times of the Buddha, Mistry's *Siddhartha* is refreshingly contemporary, set in a vipassana meditation centre in the Western Ghats. Technology and spirituality are inextricably linked. The main teacher, long dead, lives on as a booming voice on the audio system and as an image on the TV screen. The meditators are not striving for nirvana, but seeking relief from their phobias, headaches and stomach troubles. With 352 protagonists speaking in first person 'we', *Siddhartha* is as much a spiritual tour de force (along the lines of *The Magic Mountain* by Thomas Mann) as it is an astonishingly successful literary experiment.

Question: Hormuz, we expected to find you in the middle of a forty-day vipassana shivir…

Answer: Yes, instead you find me as the proprietor of a real-estate firm in Thane.

Question: Have you stopped writing?

Answer: You make it sound like a bad thing!

Question: You knocked Hesse's *Siddhartha* off the pedestal. You owe it to the world to knock some more dead white men off their pedestals.

Answer: (Laughs) Ironically, I hadn't even read the original *Siddhartha* until after I finished writing my book. It was embarrassing.

Question: Hesse's book or the fact that you hadn't read it?

Answer: His book.

Question: See you at the literature festival.

Spandak Mazumdar, *MmYum's*, Gharonda Publishers, 2002

A mascot-clown breaks the laws of sentience and comes alive in the downtown Mumbai branch of a multinational fast-food chain. In a thinly veiled satire on the big M, Spandak avoids the usual tropes and zeroes in on the humanity of a plasto-plastic entity. Arnold MmYum narrowly escapes becoming entangled in the conspiracy of a tribe of anti-globalization activists. But the second Arnold that comes alive isn't as lucky. He is lugged off to an anti-port rally to be burned before an audience of thousands. Once Spandak's Arnolds encounter each other on the Ferozpur Janata Express, the two non-human protagonists undertake a deeply human journey of exploring the whys and hows of their own consciousness. The dawning of wisdom is slow and painful, and by the end of *MmYum's*, Spandak has masterfully depicted the whole of humanity as a bunch of clowns struggling to grasp the reasons for their sentience.

Question: Spandak, what are you doing these days?

Answer: Not writing, obviously.

Question: Why have you agreed to come to the One-hit-wonder Literature Festival?

Answer: Because I've never been to a literature festival, I published my first book at a time when there wasn't so much dubious money floating around.

Question: I'll have you know, the sponsors of our festival are absolutely legit. Anyway, how do you deal with the bitterness and shame of being a one-hit-wonder novelist?

Answer: I'll have you know, I have more important things to be shameful and bitter about.

Question: Hold that thought for the festival.

Santosh Wagekar, *2BHK*, PenGwin Books, 2005

2BHK was the super-successful first book of what was meant to be a trilogy (*1BHK* and *1RK*). Santosh Wagekar never got around to writing the other two, sparking a lengthy legal battle between him and his publisher. Santosh ultimately had to cough up the advance paid for the two unwritten books. However, the scandal does not diminish the literary merit of *2BHK*—the definitive Mumbai real-estate novel. Deep and Shaloni, a newly married couple, are on the hunt for a flat in Mumbai. Each chapter heading is the address of a flat for sale. The novel gives readers an intimate glimpse of the neighbourhoods of old Mumbai. It depicts the greed, communalism and insanity that fester within benign-seeming housing societies. By the end of *2BHK*, Deep and Shaloni are nowhere close to their dream home. They have downgraded their expectations of a spacious and clean 2BHK, and are willing to settle for a 1BHK. People, even if they are fictional characters, must live somewhere. But *2BHK* makes readers realize the futility and insanity of trying to own a sliver of Mumbai's bizarre real-estate market.

Question: Santosh, do you finally own your dream home?

Answer: *2BHK* wasn't autobiographical. I've been living in the same home for the past eighteen years.

Question: *1RK* was going to be the title of your third book in the trilogy. Do you think life is possible in a one-room-kitchen?

Answer: If I had a sea-facing 1RK at the southern tip of Mumbai, with NCPA and Marine Drive within spitting distance, then yes, I think I could raise generations there.

Question: You still seem keenly tuned in to real estate. Why not just write the damn books?

Answer: That matter is no longer sub judice, but it was for such a long time that I instinctively give circuitous responses to avoid answering what is actually a pretty straightforward question.

Question: So again, why not just write the damn books?

Answer: Because Deep and Shaloni migrated to Toronto.

Question: Have they managed to buy a house there?

Answer: They're divorced. Okay? They're effing divorced.

Question: See you at the festival!

Mithya Goswami, *In Gandhiji's Dhoti*, PaperPoppins Publications, 1991

In Gandhiji's Dhoti is the heart-wrenching story of Jhinsi, a girl compelled to leave her village and work in a middle-class household in the town of Aurangabad. As Jhinsi comes to terms with her new positioning in the class ladder, she unearths a secret about her employers that makes her realize the emptiness at the heart of the middle-class dream. Jhinsi's failure to return to her village was recognized and heralded by critics as an analogy of the irreversible effects of urbanization on billions of lives the world over. (The book takes its title from a risqué game Jhinsi and her cousins used to play in her village.) *In Gandhiji's Dhoti* was translated into eleven foreign languages. The novel was shortlisted for the Eliza Rahmani First Book Prize and the Ekwata Kayoli Book Award.

Question: Mithya, what are you doing these days?

Answer: I am a successful and contented home-furnishing retailer in Aurangabad.

Question: When are you publishing your next book?

Answer: Soon, I hope. But I don't know. Some days I feel I just don't have it in me. On other days, I'll be talking to some wholesaler or buying vegetables at the market and suddenly the second book will feel as real as someone standing next to me. I just don't know.

Question: Don't you want to carry forward the legacy of your first book?

Answer: I tried to, for several years. But writing *In Gandhiji's Dhoti* brought closure to so many things I had been wanting to say. Maybe I have nothing left to say.

Question: What are your expectations from the One-hit-wonder Literature Festival?

Answer: (Laughs) A full-on experience of unbridled humiliation?

For more invitees and schedule info, log on to www.onehitwonderliteraturefestivalindia.orgy

Acknowledgements

'Engglishhh©' first appeared in *Caravan*, April 2012; 'An Indian Porn Director's Speech to His Hesitant Leading Lady' first appeared in *First Proof 2, The Penguin Book of New Writing*, 2006, and *India* (ISBN Edizioni, Italy, 2008); 'Nice Water' first appeared in *India* (ISBN Edizioni, Italy, 2008); 'The Watchman' first appeared in *Mumbai Noir*, Akashic Books, 2012, and HarperCollins *Publishers* India, 2012; 'Polo (the mint with the…)' first appeared in *Mad In India*, Tendance Floue, 2008; 'Mischief in Neta Nagar' first appeared in OutOfPrintMagazine.co.in, December 2011 and *New Reflections 2013*, Aschehoug Publishing House, Norway; 'The Thirteenth Floor' first appeared in *Outlook India*, 2008; 'Siddhartha' first appeared in *Tehelka*, January 2009 and *Excess: The Tehelka Book of Short Stories*, Hachette India, 2010.

Many thanks to Karthika V.K. and Bidisha at HarperCollins India.

And full marks to Anil M. at TIS for… yet again!

About the Author

Altaf Tyrewala is the author of the critically acclaimed books *No God in Sight* and *Ministry of Hurt Sentiments*. He is also the editor of the crime-fiction collection *Mumbai Noir*. His works have been published and anthologized around the world. He was awarded the 2011 DAAD Artist-in-Berlin literature grant. He lives in Mumbai with his family and works in the e-learning industry.

